WAYFARERS' HYMNS

Novels by the same author

Ways of Dying (1995)
She Plays with the Darkness (1995)
The Heart of Redness (2000)
The Madonna of Excelsior (2002)
The Whale Caller (2005)
Cion (2007)
Black Diamond (2009)
The Sculptors of Mapungubwe (2013)
Rachel's Blue (2014)
Little Suns (2015)
The Zulus of New York (2019)

ZAKES MDA

WAYFARERS' HYMNS

UMUZI

Published in 2021 by Umuzi, an imprint of Penguin Random House South Africa (Pty) Ltd
Company Reg. No. 1953/000441/07
The Estuaries No. 4, Oxbow Crescent, Century Avenue, Century City, 7441, South Africa
PO Box 1144, Cape Town, 8000, South Africa
www.penguinrandomhouse.co.za

© 2021 Zakes Mda

First edition, first printing 2021
1 3 5 7 9 8 6 4 2

ISBN 978-1-4152-1082-6 (Print)
ISBN 978-1-4152-1089-5 (e-Pub)
Cover design by Gretchen van der Byl
Text design by Nazli Jacobs
Set in Photina

Printed by **novus print**, a division of Novus Holdings

MIX
Paper from
responsible sources
FSC
www.fsc.org
FSC® C022948

1

The death of Famole
The birth of boy-child

She was the one I sang my hymns to, Moliehi, child of my mother. Though she was not there to hear them with her own ears, they told her when they returned from the mines of Welkom, Rustenburg and Johannesburg that hey, Moliehi, your name is famous among travellers and their lovers. Your name and your beauty. Drunken men and women perform to your name at famo parties. They dance the focho dance to your poppy-seed beauty. They make love to it. The accordion goes maniacal when the kheleke – the eloquent one, the one who can compose verse at the bat of an eyelid – describes you against the background of the valleys and the rivers and the fountains and the hills and the deep dongas that cut ruthlessly through the land, leaving it wounded and bleeding.

She only smiled shyly when she heard these stories and carried on with her life as if the fame meant nothing to her. As if it was about someone else. As if she was just an ordinary village girl whose brother was not a revered kheleke.

That is what a sister means to any boy-child who is a singer of hymns. Lifela tsa litsamaea-naha; lifela tsa liparola-thota. The hymns of those who traverse the land; those who roam the valleys. Woe unto a kheleke who has no sister, for the best he can do is sing about his paternal aunt, his rakhali, unless there is another formidable woman in his life. Provided it is not his wife. No self-respecting kheleke sings the praises of his wife in public, lest he invite vultures to his homestead while he rambles the land to the rhythm of the accordion and drums. But a sister, yes.

A great hymn begins with the kheleke introducing himself to the world, repeating his name and his father's, against his father's if his father was a reprobate as men tend to be, and praising the virtues of his clan, his village and his chief. The lie of the land and its overwhelming beauty are never left out, even when the hymn is a lamentation. Even when the land is barren. There is beauty in starkness. And then the sister. A kheleke dwells on his sister and her unsurpassed qualities of womanhood. Especially if she does not stand any rubbish from any man. Like Moliehi. I, boy-child, often add in mock lamentation, Oh, Moliehi, lioness of the Bataung clan, the dark one from my mother's womb, Mmantšo, unlike most of her clan who are descendants of Barwa and are therefore yellow-coloured, how will I ever get cattle through you when you're so full of shit?

She was the one whose beauty I sang about. Moliehi, khaitseli ea motho. And then she was lying there with a gaping wound on her head.

They could have killed her, said the male officer. And then he added after a pause, If they wanted to.

They obviously wanted you to see her like this, said the female officer. In pain. Not dead, but almost. Perhaps they wanted her to die in your arms so that you feel the pain more acutely.

6

Twisting the knife in my heart while her wound was pulsating as if she was breathing through it. If there was the slightest breath, whether through the nostrils, the mouth or the gaping wound, there was hope of life.

They had no name. The officers obviously knew who *they* were. The officers knew their methods too. They killed when they wanted to. Or they just gave you a few whacks with a panga and left you at death's door so that your kin could learn a lesson. Stop your shit once and for all, that's what they were saying, or the subject of your hymns – the object of your love, khaitseli ea motho, she whose name you repeated over and over, invoking protective female spirits as you rambled over hills and hillocks even from the days the concertina was your instrument instead of the accordion – will die for real next time.

We'll do our best, said the doctor.

Reassurance was proffered by Toloki, the Professional Mourner, the votary I first met during the days of the concertina.

Be joyful, boy-child, he said, or at least be relieved. I do not mourn the living. Only the dead.

*

The concertina keened across the gorges and was echoed by boulders on the hills and cliffs on the mountains. Even the rock rabbits stirred, and women gathering firewood in the bush stopped their gossip and paid attention to the song undulating from the bellows. They must have muttered, there he goes, the boy-child whose body will end up being food for the vultures, Moliehi's brother, there he goes, giving himself to the land.

Usually, giving myself to the land meant rambling, without any specific destination, heading where the wind blew me, until the smell of fermented sorghum stopped me in my tracks and led me to a place of abandon where buxom women performed focho, the dance that young South Africans have appropriated and call vosho. This time it is different. The road has a destination. It leads to Matelile Ha Sekhaupane. To pay my last respects to Famole, the greatest singer of hymns who ever lived.

Opinions will differ, of course, as they differ on everything else in life, but I have long worshipped at the altar of Famole. He was the greatest both in making the accordion moan with pleasure as his fingers tickled it and in the manner that he selected his words so that they went straight to your heart. Famole, in my opinion, was more talented than all hymn singers, including his own mentor, Mantša Mohale. But I am only allowed to whisper this out of ear-shot of some people in our villages of Matelile, Likhoele and Thabana Morena, which are pulsating with rival musicians, or even in our whole district of Mafeteng that is populated by followers who take such matters personally. Giving such praise to a singer of hymns can be a death sentence if the listeners are supporters of a different musician. I still want to live.

They say Famole prophesied his own death. The last CD he released contained a lamentation titled 'Lebitla le Nkemetse' – the grave is waiting for me – that followers (they prefer to be called followers – balateli – rather than fans) played over and over again because it spoke so directly of his final journey. After a searing accordion and drums that throb with the heartbeat, his voice – in a phefa tone, as Basotho would say when they describe the clarity and mellifluous-ness of a voice – creeps in and repeats that the grave awaits him, awaits him, awaits him. Jo nna oeee! He proceeds to sing that he knows for sure that the grave is waiting for him. Then he gets to the hymn part of the song where he recites poetry in that modulated space that exists between talking and singing. The sing-song voice of an accomplished kheleke backed by a demented accordion. He tells us that everyone is born already with the number of his grave. But no one knows his or her number except Father God. He tells his followers they should not be angry or sad, for they are going to meet him in heaven. His final wish is that his old-time mentor, Mantša Mohale, should be the speaker who passes condolences at his funeral.

Jo nna oeee, these songs talk! Maybe that's why their poetry is called lifela – hymns. Nothing to do with church hymns, though. These are secular hymns that suppliants dance to. Most of the hymns, even from their origins, never had anything to do with religion. Famole's swansong, of course, had a touch of religion because it was about his impending death.

And people spoke at that funeral, each trying to outdo the one who spoke before. Basotho are a speaking people; they value the music that words strung together with care and love can produce and are competitive in the originality of their metaphors. People spoke, some calling him by his birth name, Teboho Lesia, to show that they knew him long before he was Famole, when he was still a herdboy looking after his father's cattle, when his mother was an ardent believer of the Anglican Church, and how that instilled the love of Christianity in him. And, of course, his apprenticeship to the mentor of many musicians, Mantša Mohale.

The mentor was really the person I was waiting to hear as I stood at the margins of the funeral crowd, my concertina hidden under my donkey blanket, so named because of its grey colour. I observed people in different-coloured blankets. People were obviously not afraid to wear their colours because of the strong presence of the police and the military. The police from the nearby Ha Seeiso Police Station had been reinforced by those from the district headquarters of Mafeteng, and by a few officers from the Lesotho Defence Force. The pretext was that law enforcement was here because of the heavy presence of government officials and political leaders. To look after their safety. But everyone knew that the main reason was to quell any fight that might arise from rival groups. A cynic might say even to take sides, as people have always said politicians and their minions are not neutral in this war of the musicians.

We wear our blankets even in the hottest of summers, hence most of the people here were in their colourful blankets, ranging from the thick qibi blanket, otherwise known as serope sa motsoetse – a nursing mother's thigh – because of its warmth, to the ornate seana-marena, lefitori and letlama. All these are just elegant blankets to the rest of the Basotho nation, but here in Matelile and in Thabana Morena, the homes of famo musicians, and perhaps in the district of Mafeteng, these blankets, and especially their colours, represent feuding factions.

At the margins of the crowd, close to where I was standing, I spotted a strange-looking couple. Neither was wearing blankets of any kind, which made them stand out. But it was what the man was wearing that made him even more conspicuous. A black cape and a black top hat. The pants and shoes were also black. He was quite short and broad-shouldered, with a yellow-coloured face and sorrowful eyes that were glassy with unshed tears. Perhaps one of Famole's followers from the Land of Gold, people nearby speculated. Perhaps himself a musician. You know how musicians like to call attention to themselves by dressing and behaving differently from the rest of humanity. He could not be from here. The woman too looked strange, but in a normal way. She was tall, dwarfing the man, and carried herself with so much dignity you would think she was the reincarnation of Queen 'Mamohato, the queen-mother who passed on a year before. Except for the fact that the queen-mother was of a much shorter stature than this long-limbed beauty and would certainly be wearing a blanket like all her subjects.

I was staring at this strange couple when Mantša finally took the podium and spoke the words that later became his popular recording called 'Lerumo la Nthlaba' – the spear has stabbed me.

Jo nna!! Jonana oeee! A spear has stabbed me, he wailed to the sound of the accordion and drums. The death of Famole has touched me so painfully. Where do you go when you feel the pain? The child of Lesia has left us. Then Mantša wept like a woman. No, not just wept, he wailed like a widow after being informed of the death of her husband. Then he spoke the hymn part of the song, the sing-song poetry, repeating that the spear had stabbed him in the heart, and consoling the children of Lesia and all Famole's followers. He went on to appeal to the chief of the area, Morena Selomo, to look after Famole's children, so that their life was as good as when Famole was still alive. He ended his hymn by warning Famole's wife not to listen to people's gossip but to focus on raising Famole's children.

It was as if he knew that gossip would begin even before people left the funeral that day. When I, boy-child, was in the queue to wash my hands in the water mixed with aloe, part of funeral etiquette, the people behind me could not stop jabbering about which funeral orator was good, which one lied, how did the Nurse know how Famole died since he was not in that car accident, or if it was true at all that Famole died in a car accident and was not killed by rival gangsters.

This one about the Nurse was nit-picking really. We all know that these days the Nurse at a funeral can be any orator who can share the details of how the deceased died, not necessarily someone who was personally there as a nurse – mooki – when the deceased was sick, as it originally used to be.

We of the margins were served samp in a big basin, I suspect someone's bathtub though no one would ever confess to that, or it was just my ungenerous thought, and a whole mountain of meat in yet another giant basin. We dug in with our own hands, while a man with an accordion played what passed for a church hymn. I noticed that the strange couple was sitting on the grass, a few feet away, and was not partaking of the food. Perhaps they felt they deserved to be in the tent where important people ate from plates with spoons, knives and forks, and even had green salads, chakalaka and beetroot. Perhaps where they came from they were not people of the margins like us.

The gossip continued about Famole's death. He didn't die like a warrior in war, a man said. Anybody can die in a car accident. Nothing special about it. It seemed the gossips despised Famole for dying in a mere car accident instead of being mowed down by the bullets of rival musicians.

I could not hold myself any more. You, I yelled, who are you to hate a man because he died a peaceful death?

A car accident is not peaceful, said one of them, with a what-business-is-it-of-yours sneer in both his voice and on his face.

You despise him because he did not die in a gunfight. You heard from funeral orators that he was a gentle soul, not involved in the war of the musicians.

The gossip broke into a mocking laughter. You pretend that Famole was holy, he said. Yet he was one of the leaders of MaRussia gangs in Soweto. Ask anyone from Senaoane, Phiri and Mapetla. They will tell you he was a gang leader.

When the funeral scones and the gemmer, or ginger beer, were brought, the gossip became even more animated, crunching the hard scones with the noise of an industrial grinder. I glanced at the strange couple. Now they too were eating the hard scones. They were dunking them in the gemmer first, hoping to soften them. You don't mess with funeral scones.

You can't tell lies about a man in his own homestead at his own funeral, I said in disgust.

It was Famole these clowns were talking about; the man on whose hymn-singing career I aimed to model mine. Thebe e seheloa holim'a enngoe. A new shield is stencilled from an old one. Everything is built on something that came before it.

Take it from me, mate, there is no musician who is totally clean of blood.

Another man, wearing a similar-coloured blanket, added, It is the money, the recording contracts that make them insane.

It is jealousy, said the gossip. Jealousy eats them all.

A Mosotho does not want to see another Mosotho succeed, declared his friend.

Not Famole, I said. He was the most successful. He was well trained by Mantša, who is also a man of peace.

Was it not this very Famole who shot Khosi Mosotho Chakela because Chakela was now overtaking him in popularity?

I knew that story. Everyone in Matelile, Likhoele and Thabana Morena knew that story. Chakela claimed that he was shot by Famole in Phiri, Soweto, and had to escape to his headquarters in Bloemfontein where his people nursed him back to health. Brought him back almost from the throes of death. I never believed that Famole was capable of such brutality, judging from the gentleness of his music. And if you heard the wonderful things they were saying about him at his funeral you wouldn't believe it either. I am not saying Chakela was lying when he accused Famole. I am saying maybe, just maybe, he was mistaken. Maybe it was not Famole but somebody who looked like him. Maybe the gangs used Famole's name to terrorise Chakela out of Phiri. Maybe. Maybe.

Canonise Famole all you want, said the gossip, leaving me standing there, obviously to equip himself with more hard scones. Funeral scones are toothsome even though they tax your teeth. They tempt you to crunch one after another till your stomach threatens to burst.

My curiosity about the strange couple got the better of me and I worked my way towards them. I greeted and sat down without waiting for them to invite me to join them.

Famole's friends, I guess? I asked.

We know his music, said the man. What you people here call hymns. But we never met the man.

Hymns are the recitation part of the music, the rap part, the sing-song poetry part. Of course, the whole song can be a hymn from the beginning to the end if it all comprises poetry and accordion.

Thank you for the lesson, said the man. I was not sure whether he was being sarcastic or genuine. I didn't mean it to sound like a lesson.

You must have really loved his hymns for you to come all the way for his funeral, I said, hoping they would tell me where all the way was.

I am Toloki the Professional Mourner, the man said.

I think the woman saw the puzzlement on my face. She came to the rescue and said, Toloki mourns the dead. The bereaved pay him to sit on the mound to mourn the deceased.

She is Noria, the love of my life, said Toloki. The only lover I have ever had from the time I was a kid back in our village. She, on the other hand, has a different story.

That is oversharing, said Noria. The man did not ask for our history.

I'm sure it's an interesting history, I said. But this business of being paid to mourn is difficult for me to understand. The bereaved mourn

14

for themselves and the whole community mourns with them; why would they pay someone to do it for them?

Toloki cleared his throat and adopted a sermonic tone. Where death is plentiful, the community gets exhausted by mourning, he said. They merely go through the motions to fulfil expectations, but their hearts are not really in it. A professional mourner relieves them of the burden of mourning. Of course, in this part of the world they must first learn how my services can be of great use to them since professional mourning is not part of their tradition. It was like that too in the coastal city from which we have migrated. At first they said ubuntu would not allow them to pay someone to mourn for them because they believed that they, their friends and their relatives had the obligation and the capacity to mourn for one another's deaths. But soon enough, because death was so plentiful as a result of political upheavals, I was doing a roaring trade mourning for victims of different kinds of death. There are many ways of dying.

Then why did you leave? I asked. Did death get finished?

Even at this funeral I have heard your people say death is the daughter-in-law of all homesteads, Toloki said. This means that death lives with us every day. It will never get finished as long as human beings exist. Of course, in our coastal city deaths are fewer than they were in the days when people were fighting for freedom and were therefore killing one another in their hundreds. But there is still enough of it to keep me busy for years to come.

I think Toloki is bored with mourning in the same townships for so many years, said Noria.

Yes, I am in search of new deaths, new ways of dying and new ways of mourning.

That was why he came to this area that encompasses such villages as Matelile, Thabana Morena and Likhoele – all famous throughout southern Africa for the musicians they have produced. But now notorious because of the wars among musicians which happen mostly at the gold and platinum mines of South Africa, but overflow to these villages since they are the origins of the musicians who then must be buried at their ancestral homes.

We came to mourn here because these are different deaths from those we have been used to. Death by music.

Where we come from music uplifts, said Noria. Here it kills. I decided Toloki should set up camp here for some time and mourn the musicians and their followers. Until he has had his fill. Then we'll move on to the next destinations that will give us more exciting ways of mourning.

It occurred to me that Noria, who Toloki said was the love of his life, was also his manager.

Music that kills. Music to die for. Music to die to.

*

Quite often I broke away from the group. Unintentionally. My gait was controlled by the music of the concertina. It is not for nothing that it is known as the music of those who traverse the land. It makes your legs hungry for the land and its pathways. It makes your feet eat the grass as it begins to peep above the soil, leaving the path bald again. The people in the group did not have the stride for this kind of walking. The younger ones tried to keep up, singing along with me and my concertina. The older ones remained behind, perhaps saying, Let him leave us, our joints are no longer meant for this kind of show-off. We'll find him on the way.

But it was not for show-off. It was the fuel that emanated from my fingers.

Sooner or later we would stop and wait for the slacking group to catch up. Especially the two members who were my guests – Toloki and Noria. The rest had their own destinations and were with us only for the company. They soon branched off and headed for their villages. Until I was left with only Toloki and Noria, negotiating our way up the mountains, across the Thabana Morena Plateau, between cornfields and down escarpments, until after six hours or so we reached Likhoele.

The chickens were roosting already, and if you know our village, people tend to retire to their beds and sleeping mats at the same time.

Moliehi smiled at the visitors and told them they were welcome. They sat at the table and she lit a paraffin lamp for them. When she walked out of the house, I knew I had to follow her. I had detected a frown in her smile.

Bringing us visitors at this time of the night? she said. Without even telling me? What will they eat? Where will they sleep?

They will eat whatever we eat, I said. When we eat pap and sugared water, they will eat the same. They will sleep in grandma's mokhoro – her round hovel.

They are city people, are they not? I saw the way the woman is dressed.

They may be city people, I said, but they are not fussy. The man is a professional mourner. You can't be hoity-toity if you're a professional mourner.

What is that?

He travels from funeral to funeral, mourning the dead.

I explained how I met them at Famole's funeral, where I suspected they had hoped they would be allowed to ply their trade.

But people don't know them yet, I said. When they get to know them, it will be prestigious to have them at your funeral. They came to our region because they heard of the manifold deaths of musicians and their followers.

Moliehi was not impressed. These people could not be a good omen, especially since they dealt in death.

They don't deal in death, I corrected her. They don't kill anyone. They merely mourn those who have been killed by others. I invited them to come with me when they mentioned they might have to trek to Malealea Lodge to sleep there. Visitors cannot sleep at a hotel when there is a mokhoro that no one uses except grain and rats. They can stay with us while they set themselves up. After all, I am setting myself up too. We can find our way together.

Moliehi gave that mocking laugh that consigned everything I said to the realm of pipe dreams. I walked back to the house to pump the Primus stove and serve the visitors hot sugarless rooibos tea and yesterday's sorghum bread.

They repeatedly thanked me for my kindness and assured me that it was no big deal that our accommodation was meagre – which is how I described it as I apologised for it being many grades below Malealea Lodge.

They were curious to know more about me and my obsession with Famole.

My obsession is really with music, I told them. Famole is merely the kind of musician I would like to be. I started with harmonica, like most village boys, when I looked after my father's cattle. When he was alive and still had cattle. Before the table fell on him in one of the deepest gold shafts in Johannesburg. When they were puzzled about a falling table, I explained to them that it meant when the rocks collapse and trap the miners underground. Often they are never rescued but die there and we say the table has fallen on them. They cannot be buried among their kin in the ancestral land and their spirits remain unappeased. Part of the wandering spirits of African children that seek redress.

That's what happened to my father, and soon after that debtors took most of his cattle and rustlers helped themselves to the rest.

After joining at NRC – the Native Recruitment Corporation – and becoming a miner myself the first thing I bought with my first salary was a concertina. I taught myself how to play, but played it mostly for myself, or for a few drinkers at the hostel. I never really played professionally at the famo parties. Its tone was too emaciated for famo parties. The accordion had by then taken over as the instrument of famo and focho. Accordion and home-made drums.

They listened wistfully as I told them that one day I would buy my own accordion. Moliehi shook her head. My dream was not her dream. She didn't say anything this time because she didn't want to be disagreeable in the presence of visitors. She would rather I went back to the mines to dig gold and platinum like other upright men and pay bohali for a good woman and settle down in a blissful marriage. According to her, musicians were scallywags and vaga-bonds who led immoral lives in perpetual drinking parties. And then they fight and kill one another. For her, this brother of hers, this boy-child who was not only the only brother but the only sibling, should not die in the gutter with bullet wounds like some of the musicians of this area.

But Moliehi, child of my mother, also knew how stubborn I was. How I really wanted to live my dream.

You can be anything you want to be, said Toloki.

Haven't we heard such platitudes before? asked Moliehi.

I am going to inherit Famole's throne, I announced, stressing every syllable. Before my body is pulled apart by vultures I, boy-child, will be the new Famole.

2

Days of the concertina

Toloki turned out to be a very moody man when there was no funeral to attend. There was no shortage of funerals in our region, comprising the great villages of Likhoele, Matelile and Thabana Morena, also known as the Accordion Triangle. There were always funerals because death lived with us every day. Not only the deaths of musicians and their followers mowed down with AK-47 rounds, but the deaths of sinewy men when tunnels collapsed on them inside the mines of South Africa, or the deaths of men and women in the prime of their youth eaten to the bone by Aids, phthisis or tuberculosis. You heard already that lefu ke ngoetse ea malapa ohle. Death is the daughter-in-law of all homesteads.

Toloki's body yearned to mourn when there was no client willing to buy into this new-fangled concept of professional mourning. When he offered his services for free – both to satisfy his craving and to demonstrate to the bereaved, present and future, what his profession entailed and how it would enrich their funerals – but was shooed away by the sceptics, he paced the floor and mumbled some chant to himself. The suppressed sounds were like the noises he normally made at the beginning of his routine at the graveside before he lunged into full-throttled mourning. I heard this at the two funerals I attended with him and watched in awe as he sat on a mound and whined like a wild dog on heat and trilled like mating cats and howled like an orgasmic philanderer.

But this time the chant was under his breath. Still I could hear and identify it. And it sent shivers through my body as if it was itself portending death.

The pacing irritated Moliehi and she demonstrated that by fetching a broom from the main house and sweeping the ground in front of Toloki, raising so much dust that it made him cough.

She, child of my mother, still had not come to terms with the presence of these votaries at my father's homestead. She was known to never reserve her views or feelings for the next day. She showed you her colours there and then. Even the neighbours knew her temper and would tell me, Jo, that Moliehi of yours; she doesn't say tomorrow!

The visitors knew that she was not a willing hostess.

We are not wanted here, we better move on, Toloki told me one day.

I should have been happy. I should have taken advantage of this offer and said yes, maybe indeed it is time to go. But I felt bad and assured him that Moliehi would soon come around. She just was not used to company.

You can't just rush away before you are able to set up on your own and mourn plentiful death to your heart's content, I said.

Noria kept herself in the background like a shadow. She preferred to sit among the bags of grain in the mokhoro hut even when the sun was shining and the whole village was basking in it. Occasionally she called out, Toloki! Especially when his pacing in the clearing between the round hovel and the main house was getting to be too annoying even to her. Toloki would respond, Yes, Mother of Vutha, and rush into the hut. He called her that whenever he wanted to appease her. Mother of Vutha.

Toloki would remain in the hut with his beloved and there would be peace in the world. But after an hour or two he would burst out of the mokhoro, bask in the sun with me for a while, and then start pacing and mumbling again.

When are your friends leaving? Moliehi asked one Saturday, a question I was now used to.

Soon I hope, I said.

She knew I was lying.

Her impatience was beginning to prevail on me, and I kept on promising that the following week I would give them a week's notice to leave.

Next week next week next week, she repeated. Do you think I am a child? You have been saying next week next week for a month now.

At least they are contributing something for their keep which both of us enjoy sharing, I said.

We were fine without them, said Moliehi. We were not exactly starving.

We were not starving at all, thanks to her. She was the one who kept my father's fields alive. She joined village work-parties called matsema to work on other people's fields. When it was her turn, the community joined hands to work on the two fields the old man left us when the Balimo called him to join them. She cultivated beans, peas, potatoes and maize. In winter she even tried her hand at wheat. She sold some of the harvest to the general dealer's store here at Likhoele or even at Fraser's at the camp in Mafeteng, depending on who was giving her a better price. She stored some bags in the mokhoro for us to eat for the rest of the year. Toloki and Noria slept with those bags and did whatever they did at night amongst our food.

Their contribution is important, I said. You can't dismiss it.

She just clicked her tongue against her teeth, mncm, a dismissive gesture that could be translated in words to Bullshit!

I was right about enjoying the delicacies that the votaries shared with us. At least I did, even if Moliehi did not or pretended not to.

Toloki often bought a packet of Pret, the hard vegetable cooking fat that Moliehi put in the beans she cooked to make them tastier. When he was happy, he bought Holsum, a much better quality brand of cooking fat that made food taste like meat. Holsum was particularly good in the theepe wild spinach that Noria went to pick between the fields. On weekends Toloki bought either Lucky Star or Glenryck pilchards in tomato sauce which Noria fried in curry with tomato and onion to increase the amount, and we ate it with pap. Once he came with a can of khomo-boleke – a cow in a can – which is what we called canned corned beef. Noria fried it with onion, though it was pre-cooked already.

You must admit that since these visitors came, we eat like chiefs instead of the commoners that we are, I said to Moliehi.

That's why you don't want them to leave, you greedy bastard, said Moliehi shaking her head as if she pitied me.

I broke into laughter and said, If I'm a bastard then that says something about our mother.

Initially Moliehi would be reluctant to eat this food. When Toloki and Noria were there she would pretend not even to touch their food. But as soon as they disappeared into the mokhoro for the night she would gormandise the food quickly and clean her lips so that she looked as innocent as the day she was born.

When Moliehi went to work in our father's fields I wandered from hamlet to hamlet plying my concertina music at good-time places. I couldn't stray too far because it would be rude to leave Moliehi alone with the visitors for the whole night. That was the only reason I sometimes felt their presence held me hostage. My feet were crying for the pathways of our vast wilderness, some of which I was sure were already growing grass since I was no longer stamping on them to the rhythm of my concertina.

These were days of the concertina.

I was labelled a lazy leloabe by the rest of the Likhoele community. People said I was afraid of work, otherwise why had I not returned to the mines to dig the White man's gold from the intestines of the earth like all the young men of my age, or why was I not helping Moliehi to look after the fields? Indeed, they said, if I were a real man the cattle that my father left with us when he went bōea-batho, the place where we'll all go never to return, would still be there giving us more calves and plenty of milk. But all I did was wander from one famo party to the next playing the no-good concertina, until my father's wealth was finished.

They were just echoing Moliehi.

I had never seen myself as a leloabe, or vagabond, but as a mole-lere, or wanderer. There is a big difference. And we fought about it with Moliehi, khaitseli ea motho, the very day Toloki was mumbling. She said that like a typical leloabe I had gathered fellow maloabe – by which she meant Toloki and Noria – to set up camp at her father's homestead, and that if I was a proper man like her father was – as if he was not my father too – I would be at the platinum mines of Rustenburg or the gold mines of Welkom working for the future of my children.

I don't have children, I said with much glee.

24

And you're proud of that? Your coevals have wives and home-steads of their own. They have cattle and fields and children by the dozen.

I was saved by a neighbour who hollered a greeting from the pile of boulders that used to comprise my father's cattle corral. I hollered back my response, calling him by his clan name. He enquired after our well-being. Toloki always ignored such greeting and carried on with whatever he was doing, which was considered uncouth by the community. But the more forgiving villagers said, what do you expect from a strange man like that? His ways are different. His customs are not of this world. Didn't they say he is paid to mourn the deaths of strangers? Perhaps where he comes from people are not greeted.

You heard about Mme Mpuse? the neighbour asked.

What about her? I asked, betraying a slight panic.

A question framed like that could only mean something bad had happened to her. Puseletso Seema, or Mme Mpuse to those who loved her, was a hymn singer of note who was famous in all of southern Africa as she had been recording her music from the early days of vinyl to the days of the cassette tape and right up to these days of the compact disc. She continued to be the most famous female singer of the seoeleoelele music, as her hymn singing is called because of the repetition of those words. Once upon a time she was the most famous hymn singer, male or female, full stop. She had since been overtaken by quite a few male singers, including Khosi Mosotho Chakela and the recently deceased Famole and his ageing mentor Mantša. She had also been a gun-toting gangster for many years, and had married one gang boss after another, mostly from the deadly MaRussia gangs, and all her three or four husbands had died by the gun. It was reasonable of me to fear that she had come to a sticky end.

She is here, said the neighbour. She arrived in the village last night. Musicians are gathered at her father's homestead to welcome her home.

I was annoyed that he introduced such good news by first alarming me with a stupid question.

She has not been in Likhoele for years, I said. Her father's house has become ruins ever since she left abruptly. I wonder what she is back here for?

She is doing some work, said the neighbour. Mosebetsi oa balimo. Some rituals for the ancestors. She asked after you. She thought you were at the mines, but I told her you were still a leloabe here in Likhoele with your concertina.

Mme Mpuse was the pride of our Likhoele village. Though she herself claimed to have been born in Newclare, Johannesburg, her father was born and bred here. His compound stood here for years even when he worked at Makhooeng, in the land of the White man, which was what we continued to call South Africa even long after Mandela had taken over as president and members of parliament were by far majority Black. Until his death he returned every December to celebrate Christmas with his kin, one of whom was not Puseletso Seema since those days she had been swallowed by Makhooeng where she was both a singer and a gangster's moll, and later a gangster in her own right. The more pious of the villagers called her a letekatse la MaRussia – a whore of the MaRussia gangs. Only when she was famous with some records to her name did we see her occasionally visiting her father's compound with her Ma-Russia men. And only after all her husbands were serially mowed down by rival gangs did she return to rebuild her father's homestead and take refuge in it. But soon she left, claiming that the villagers were stealing from her and wanted to bewitch her. She was given refuge by the Principal Chief of Matsieng, Prince Bereng Seeiso, King Letsie II's brother himself, at Lower Qeme where she established a permanent home for herself and her grandchildren.

I went into the main house, threw a lefitori blanket over my shoulder, placed a mokorotlo hat on my head and grabbed my concertina. I invited Toloki to come with me to pay homage to Mme Mpuse. He invited Noria to join us. Moliehi, though normally not a lover of things, invited herself and came along. After all, it was Mme Mpuse we were talking about. She knew her music from the FM radio but had never seen her. Curiosity got the better of her.

The music of accordions met us on the way even before Mme Mpuse's homestead came in sight. The stamping feet of the lihoba dancers shook the earth. We arrived to the competing harmonies of about four accordions and one concertina. A man and a woman were playing home-made drums created from metal containers with car tube rubber for the drumhead. The woman drummer found much joy in tickling the makeshift cymbals made of rows of Coca-Cola and Fanta bottle tops. I had never seen any of the musicians before, but I took it that they were amateurs from the Accordion Triangle rather than her regular band, Tau ea Linare, which was more professional and played electric guitars and complete drum sets with cymbals and toms and snares and bass and all. Indeed, Mme Mpuse had lost some respect among connoisseurs of our accordion famo hymns when she went electric and introduced a regular band to back her, polluting the music of the wanderers as we knew it. We blamed the greed of the record companies who wanted to turn this revered hymn singer into a pop star like Brenda Fassie. But the people of the world continued to devour her music quite relentlessly and she danced all the way to the bank. Or so we believed. Until we discovered that thieves in the guise of managers and agents danced all the way to their own banks on her behalf.

Of course, I wouldn't be left behind, otherwise why do you think I took my concertina with me? I joined in what at first sounded like dissonance. A cacophony of notes. Soon the music gelled and held together even though none of us had rehearsed. It was more like what the jazz cats call a jam session; musicians who come together from different quarters and improvise great music without any rehearsal.

My fellow concertina player took courage from seeing my confidence as I skilfully weaved my way through the accordion players, both with my notes and my dancing. He began to dance around too. We relished the fact that the accordion players could not perform any meaningful dance with their heavy instruments. They could only move their bodies in place. We were indeed showing off even to the girls present who normally valorised accordion players and despised the puny concertina.

And there was Mme Mpuse in a circle of admirers, singing and dancing. She had grown older since the last time I saw her. And heavier. Obviously, she was eating money. She danced with the carelessness of a matriarch, shiqi shiqi, now and then throwing her leg forward in an unfulfilled focho dance, instead of raising it high as younger women would have done. The lihoba dancers a few yards behind her, all wearing white shirts and black pants with black-and-white shoes, performed their mohobelo in the slow and graceful fashion that captured the dignity of the dance.

She wailed one of her naughty hymns seoeleoelele oeee! Monn'aka ha a eo nkokotele! My husband is not home come and knock at my door. My children are not home come and knock at my door. In the middle of the night, come and knock at my door.

My concertina decided at that moment to assume a life of its own and went berserk. I jumped in front of the men with their huge accordions, some shimmering with newness, and danced in front of Mme Mpuse while my concertina snaked its slim notes among the robust ones of the accordions and the vibrations of her mischievous voice. Her face broke into a smile of recognition. I had grown up a bit since the last time I backed her hymns with my concertina at a concert at the camp of Mafeteng. But here she was, recognising the boy-child, the one whose body would be shared by vultures. I kicked my legs in front of her in keeping with her lazy dance. Maintaining the laziness so as not to appear to be showing off my youthful agility.

Seoeleoelele boy-child, she wailed, when I say come and knock at my door, I'm talking to men not boys. You would not know what to do with it when it is facing you. Jo-o-ooo! I don't want to kill some other woman's child. Jooo nna oeee boy-child, you cannot handle this woman who has had many rains fall on her body.

People knew she was referring these words to me, for she was looking me straight in the eye. They laughed at her teasing me like that. I joined the laughter too and responded as expected of any self-respecting kheleke. Hymns are at their most beautiful when it's a duel, a dialogue between man and woman.

Aooo oelele Mme Mpuse oeee, I, boy-child, food for the vultures, ngoan'a moshanyana kabela manong, I'm no longer a boy but a grown man. A grown man for others but not for you, Mme Mpuse, elder of mine, mentor of mine. You, who taught me to be a kheleke. You taught me things in their variety, but you did not teach me big things. Matters of the moseme grass mat are too big for this boy-child.

People laughed and yelled at me: Coward! Coward!

He cannot be a coward, yelled an elderly man above the laughter, he respects his elders. He has been brought up well.

Mme Mpuse turned her back on me in mock contempt and continued her song, come lovey, come and knock at my door in the middle of the night. My husband is not here, my children are not here, I am all alone, come and knock at my door.

After her performance, while the accordionists were competing among themselves and various members of the crowd were trying their vocal cords at singing the hymns in an open-mic tradition, minus the microphone, a little girl came skipping about.

Nkhono says I should call you, she said.

I knew immediately that the nkhono – grandma – who was calling me was none other than Mme Mpuse. My eyes searched for Toloki, Noria and my sister but couldn't find them at the edges of the crowd where I had left them when the demons of the famo music seized me.

I followed the girl to a tent behind one of the grass-thatched huts where Mme Mpuse held court with a group of women.

What are you doing here when other men are digging gold in the stomach of the earth? she asked even before I could formally greet her.

My eyes are on the song now, Mme Mpuse, I said. It is the only thing I can see. The hymns of the wanderers. I want to be a great kheleke like you.

Only after rains of all kinds have battered your body can you achieve any measure of greatness, said Mme Mpuse. But do not deceive yourself, I cannot be the measure.

I will die trying, Mme Mpuse, I said. And I meant it.

With a concertina? she asked. It is an instrument of our fathers. You know what they mean in Gauteng when they talk of old school? A concertina is old school. Grow up, boy, the days of the concertina are over. Sell a few of your father's cattle and buy an accordion.

We no longer have cattle in the village, said a woman I recognised as a neighbour. This one finished all his father's cattle.

Rustlers finished them, I jumped in defensively. People with bad intentions ate them.

Then he must go to Gauteng and work his bottom off for an accordion, said Mme Mpuse. He will not make the big time with a concertina. He will not get a record deal. He will not play concerts. He will not make videos. He will end up playing small focho parties in remote villages where they will pay him with a scale of beer and where women will eat him and finish him klaar.

I did not argue with her. But I knew in my heart of hearts that she was right and wrong. She was right that I would not hit the big time with a concertina. She was wrong that this boy-child would be a concertina boy for the rest of his life, eaten by women for dinner. This boy-child was going to be an accordion man, even if he had to buy an old one from a Johannesburg second-hand music store. One day soon he would press the buttons of an accordion and conquer the world. Just wait and see.

A woman, obviously part of Mme Mpuse's entourage, teased her. Ao, Mme Mpuse, is this not the Ben Ten you invited to come and knock at your door in the middle of the night?

Ao oeee, you want me to commit chicken murder, 'manyeo? said Mme Mpuse to the laughter of all the other women.

I left to join the other revellers at that point, embarrassed that they were emasculating me with their words, making me the butt of their silly jokes. It was fine when the teasing was in a song. A song was play-acting. Though singers of lifela hymns sang about their real lives, their real rulers, their real sisters, their real landscapes, their real tribulations, we all knew that when they sang about their own beauty, bravery in gun fights, prowess in stick fighting, or stamina on the moseme grass mat, for most of them it was just braggadocio. Especially when it was a competition between two hymn singers, each extolling his or her virtues. And vices. Some vices could be social currency for a kheleke.

People had finished eating and were drinking beer. Older men wearing their colourful blankets or just the grey donkey blankets were sitting in their own group, each taking a few gulps from a can of sorghum beer and then cleaning his moustache with the back of his hand as he passed the can to the next man. The women, also resplendent in colourful blankets or just covering their shoulders with bath towels or plaid shawls, sat in a group of their own, and passed the can in a similar manner, minus the moustache part. The boys in jeans, sneakers, T-shirts and baseball caps stood in their group gossiping about girls who didn't pay any attention to them but were clapping hands, singing and displaying dance moves to the glee of the group. Like the boys, none were wearing blankets. They were in floral dresses or in colourful slacks and sneakers.

I joined Toloki and Noria in a group of their own – just the two of them. They were just watching; not partaking in the beer drinking. They were no longer a curiosity. People had ogled them enough, and their eyes were now inured to the man's strangeness. Their fingers were tired of pointing at him. Yes, that's the man we have been hearing strange things about. Yes, the man who mourns the deaths of strangers.

Where is Moliehi?

She left, said Noria. She got disgusted when you started singing naughty songs with the old woman.

Well, her loss, I said.

It was time for Mme Mpuse to thank her guests. She stood on the stoep in front of a stone house and a man next to her called for order, tsie lala!

Seoeleoelele, Mme Mpuse shouted in a vibrating musical voice. People expected she would follow that with a hymn. But instead she made a speech.

My tribulations are tribulations of the world, she said. I therefore thank you for coming here to bear them with me. A burden becomes lighter when it is shared. Children of one person share even the head of a locust. However many they are, each one gets a piece.

Some man at the back yelled an encouragement, Bua, Mme Mpuse, bua! Talk, Mme Mpuse, talk.

I came here to my father's village, to my father's homestead, to slaughter for the ancestors, to talk with those who are in the ground, to tell them oeeele! you have punished me enough. I have heard. They must remove the senyama darkness that hovers over my head. They must remove the curse that steals my success.

There was utter silence. People like the news of other people, especially when it is bad. They listened expectantly, keen to know what could be bothering such a successful woman who was famous the world over and was featured on television and radio and we boasted about her among nations, you see that singer of hymns, we know her personally. She is from our village. She is known even by kings. Was it not Prince Bereng Seeiso himself who gave her accommodation at one of his villages in Qeme when she was sick and tired of us here at Likhoele? When she called us thieves and offspring of the Devil? How can such a fortunate woman talk of misfortune?

Once more she thanked the people for coming to help her get rid of her senyama or bad luck.

I made this feast to appease the ancestors. My life has been nothing but hell. God gave me the gift of song; I sing the hymns of those who traverse the valleys better than any other human being, but still senyama follows me. I do not see what I am working for. My money disappears even before it gets into my hands. I am robbed every day by malinyane a Liabolosi, the offspring of Diablo, the horned one who also goes by the name of Satan, the evil one also known as record companies. Jooo nna mme oeeeee, this child of Seema has been eaten to the bone by record companies.

I went to fight at the offices of record companies in Johannesburg. I yelled and cursed their managers. All they did was to give me a few rands to catch a train back to the township. Men of my clan stopped me when I wanted to reach for my gun, return to their offices and teach them a lesson. It was during those days when I was still a woman of the gun. Jooo nna mme oeeeee!

We hoped she would break into a hymn at this point. Or just a song. But she did not. She wanted it to be a speech so that we took her troubles seriously. So that we did not think she was just playing or teasing. Like when she invited men to come and knock at her door in the middle of the night in the absence of a husband.

The orphan that I am, Mme Mpuse continued, it is not only record companies that run away with my royalties. It is the pirates as well, those offspring of Diablo who steal my music and record it on their own tapes and CDs to sell to others. I remain poor because of pirates. That is my other senyama from which the ancestors should cleanse me.

Senyama follows me everywhere I go. I married three beautiful men. Or was it four? Not at the same time, you perverts. One after another. And one after another they died the death of the gun. My beautiful men, who were so beautiful as if they bathed in milk, who were MaRussia leaders who knew how to sing hymns, who were experts in stick fighting, who knew how to dance swinging AK-47s, were deprived of the pleasures of sorghum when they were sent to early graves. They say you live by the gun and you die by the gun. I am tired of living by the gun. I want to continue to eat sorghum. And pumpkin. Let those who are in the ground save me.

She wept.

This was a new Mme Mpuse we were seeing. The one who lamented her old days. They say ageing does that to you. It fills you with so many regrets even for those things we thought were admirable about you. These were my thoughts as I played my concertina on my way back home, thinking how I would turn those words into a song and a hymn. Toloki and Noria followed me at a respectful distance, not wanting to interfere with my musical brooding. In any event they would not have been able to keep up the pace. The concertina fuels your strides.

Outside the mokhoro hut Moliehi was cooking pap in a big three-legged cast-iron pot and beans in a smaller one.

Who is going to eat all that food? I asked. Our stomachs are still full of the meat from Mme Mpuse's work.

She just looked at me and said mncm – clicking her tongue against her teeth to express disdain. I wondered what I had done this time and went to the main house to put my blanket and concertina away. When I went back to the homestead clearing Toloki and Noria were just walking in.

You ran away from us, said Toloki.

Blame the korostina, I said.

You don't think you were too forward at Puseletso Seema's home-stead? asked Moliehi piercing me with her eyes. She did not wait for my response.

Leaping into the arena like that when no other musician was doing so, and making yourself a monkey? You embarrassed yourself.

Toloki usually stayed out of our petty quarrels, but this time he jumped right in.

Forward? he said. I thought he was wonderful.

Moliehi glared at him, her eyes saying, this is none of your business; stay out of it.

Mme Mpuse thought so too, I said, directing these words to Toloki. Then I turned to Moliehi and said, the only one who was embarrassed was you, child of my mother.

And this Puseletso Seema, the things she says! exclaimed Moliehi.

Calling her Puseletso Seema instead of the name of endearment that everyone in the village used, Mme Mpuse, I knew something negative would be coming from her mouth. I did not give her the opportunity but walked away. Toloki followed me. At the boulders that used to be a cattle corral I rolled a zol of BB Tobacco.

Ignore your sister, said Toloki. She knows you are good. She just doesn't want to say it because she doesn't want to lose you.

I drew a few puffs, contemplating his perspective.

I think you are very good, he said. We can make a great team. We should play together. I spoke about it with Noria and she thinks it's a good idea.

Play what together? I asked. You don't play anything, do you? You don't even sing hymns.

I mourn. You can play your concertina while I mourn. That will add a new touch.

I broke out in guffaws. Imagine me and my concertina making fools of ourselves mourning the dead! I, boy-child singer of the hymns of wanderers, can only feel life, not death.

I was surprised Moliehi did not dismiss the idea of my backing Toloki's mourning with my concertina. Perhaps she was warming up to this itinerant mourner and his willowy manager. I heard her that very morning grudgingly admitting that Toloki must be a good influence on me because I had stopped being a leloabe and was returning home every night. Her only concern was that my concertina might spoil the tried-and-tested effect of Toloki's performance since he was used to mourning a cappella.

I don't know if our first performance together proved her right. I was happy with it, though Toloki felt there could be some improvement.

It was a funeral of a young musician, one of those who sang makhele, the chorus that was followed by lifela hymns in the chorus-hymn-chorus structure or its variation. This was different from the masholu style of my performances which had no chorus at all, where I recited hymns throughout to instrumental accompaniment. The deceased was a chorus-boy, so to speak. Like every ambitious chorus-boy, he had hoped to graduate from makhele to masholu one day. But it was not to be. He was slain by a fellow chorus-boy in a game of dice.

I had accompanied Noria when she went to negotiate with the bereaved. After a long debate with the uncles and aunts, the family finally agreed that it would be a fitting send-off to have a professional mourner at the funeral of their child, especially if he was accompanied on the concertina – it would have been better if it was an accordion – by this boy-child who once accompanied Puseletso Seema at a concert in Mafeteng.

After the funeral the family was quite happy with our mourning. I was happy that people had seen us and were going to engage our services – or at least Toloki's services, as I had no intention of becoming part of a mourning team forever – next time they had a funeral. The itinerant mourner and the itinerant singer of the hymns of the ramblers.

I was surprised that Toloki was not totally happy.

You did well when I was sitting on the mound after people had filled in the grave and I was mourning softly, whimpering and humming the sorrows of mankind. Your harmony was very good there and it spread wonderful sorrow among the people, even those who never knew the deceased. But when I went into a crescendo, bleating like a goat being slaughtered, caterwauling like a cat on heat, you shouldn't have continued with your gentle four-part harmonies. You should have been discordant and confusing. It is that kind of ugliness that reminds us that we are going to die one day. Each one of us.

It made sense. What he was saying made total sense. He was not a maestro of mourning for nothing.

You see, we should have rehearsed as I suggested, I said.

No, you don't rehearse mourning, he said. It will never work. Just like you don't rehearse death.

Indeed, that became our method at subsequent funerals.

A day or two after the funeral of the chorus-boy I heard that Mme Mpuse was preparing to return to her homestead in Qeme as she said her grandchildren were on their own. I stole away from everyone at home and went to see her. I almost missed her; she was already loading her suitcase and big pots on the back of a bakkie. The speakers were blaring out one of her songs, the one where she is being rebellious against tradition and is backed by her band, Tau ea Linare, with electric guitars, saxophones and the like. I tried hard to listen for the accordion, and I was sad to hear it being suppressed by all those other instruments. I vowed that when I was a kheleke of the world, I would keep to the tradition of accordion and drums. I would have both makhele and masholu in my songs, but the accordion must always dominate.

Mme Mpuse gave me a surprised look.

They finished everything, my child, she said. All the meat and all the beer. And I am on the road now.

I have not come for that, Mme Mpuse. I have come for your help.

38

I told her of my quest to be a great itinerant musician and cut my own record that would make me famous and rich. That would change me from what Moliehi, child of my mother, called a leloabe, a vagabond, to a molelere, a wanderer.

Please, Mme Mpuse, introduce me to a record company, I pleaded.

She looked at me pityingly and shook her head. I thought it was because of the concertina.

I don't mean now with the concertina, I said. I will buy an accordion one of these days. I will practise and practise and practise until I am a kheleke of the world. I want to cut an album, Mme Mpuse. Mentor me. Introduce me to the record companies.

She was so annoyed with me that I thought she was going to hit me with both fists. She hit the air in front of me instead.

What is wrong with your ears, boy? she asked. Are they full of likonokono earwax? Did that silly concertina of yours make you deaf? Were you not listening to my earth-shattering speech at the feast? Were you here just to eat my meat and drink my beer instead of listening to my speech?

I was here to dance with you, I joked.

But she was in no mood for jokes.

It's not easy for me to enter the doors of those White people and their Black lackeys these days. When my blood was still hot, I threatened to shoot them, to kill them all to pieces. I no longer deal with those crooks in Johannesburg. I cut my own records now. I have my own label.

You can do that because you are already famous, I said. I didn't mean it to sound begrudging, but it did.

But you can still mentor me, I pleaded as she climbed into the bakkie and sat next to the driver. I can follow you to the ends of the earth. We can form a wonderful partnership.

The engine was roaring already.

I am too old, boy-child, she said, and her voice sounded anguished. I am too old to fight old battles. It is dangerous out there. Men with accordions and guns. Hit the pedal, driver.

The bakkie slowly moved towards the gate. I screamed after it: I, boy-child, he who will be shared by the vultures, can still be a clean musician, no guns no fighting, just the beautiful music!

Those were the days of the concertina.

3

A nostalgic hymn is echoed by the cliffs long after
the singer has departed

Our fathers, the MaRussia of the olden days, were on the payroll
of the police; today the police are on our payroll, we, the modern
MaRussia. These were words I heard quite often at good-time places
where men and women imbibed one another as much as they imbibed
the beer. I used to think it was just bombast. You know how the mix-
ture of intoxicating famo women and intoxicating beverages turned
weak men into windbags.

   No, not the part about being on the payroll of the police. That
we knew already. Though we were not yet born in the 1950s the
story is told that when the apartheid police wanted to disrupt the
Freedom Movement, they paid the MaRussia bosses in cash or in
kind – protection from the law and from other criminal syndicates –
to do it for them. For instance, when there were marches and demon-
strations and rallies, Basotho men in their colourful blankets would
descend on the congregated masses and beat them up with sjamboks
and knobkerries. Or when there was a bus strike and youths of

the Freedom Movement were shouting Azikhwelwa! stopping our mothers and fathers from getting into the PUTCO buses in protest against the high bus fares, the MaRussia would be recruited to unleash violence on any motorist who gave the strikers a ride.

Those were the innocent days when MaRussia were armed only with whips, sticks and stones. The MaRussia of today are completely different, not only in that they are followers of musicians, but because they hide machine guns from Russia – the real Russia – and from Israel, under their blankets and do not hesitate to let rounds rain. Especially on one another. The heartbeat of the drums and the moans of the accordion mix well with the crack and pop of Uzis and AK-47s.

But this thing of having the police on their payroll was fiction to me, until I saw it with my own eyes.

After Toloki bought me an accordion I took a taxi to Bloemfontein at the Mafeteng border post in search of the genius who had captured the hearts of many with his hymns. He called himself Khosi Mosotho Chakela. It was his stage name and very few knew that his real name was Rethabile Alexis Mokete. Like Famole, he was from the Matelile village. Whereas Famole was from Ha Sekhaupane, Chakela came from Ha Makhakhe, both sub-villages of Matelile. And, of course, Matelile was within the Accordion Triangle, which had birthed so many great musicians and singers of lifela tsa liparola-thota – the hymns of those who crossed gorges and valleys, who climbed mountains and waded through rivers, to share their gifts with their compatriots. And as I told you, the Accordion Triangle, is a place of rivalries, hence Chakela once accused Famole of plotting his murder.

The legend of the bad blood between Famole and Chakela did not bother me. I had nothing to do with it. After all, Famole, admittedly a hero of mine after whom I wanted to model my life, was dead. Chakela was still alive, though ageing. He could still take me under his wing and teach me greatness. That was why I worked my way to his headquarters in Bloemfontein.

I did not know how I would be received. Singers of hymns are a suspicious lot. They are always wary of spies. Spies from rival musicians. Spies from rival gangs of illegal gold miners. Spies from rival mephato – initiation and circumcision schools. Spies from law enforcement agencies on the payroll of rival syndicates. My hope was that the great man would remember my father when I told him who he was. Though he was never a musician himself, all the mines of Welkom, Johannesburg and Rustenburg knew him for his prowess in stick fighting, his reputation as a White man's trusted baas-boy and, back at the Accordion Triangle, his fame as a sehoai – a skilful farmer whose harvest was always in abundance even during the years of drought. Surely Chakela would not suspect a boy-child from the loins of such a man to have bad intentions against him.

All I knew was that Chakela lived in Bloemfontein. I thought it would be in one of the townships where Black people lived. I did not expect him to be ensconced like a White man in a suburb. But there it was, his house standing there like a citadel.

I pleaded to be allowed to see the master, but the security men – all obviously from Lesotho judging from their tongues that shaped the language with poetic aplomb and their black-and-yellow blankets that symbolised the Mafeteng district, home of Bantu Football Club – treated me like a barbarian at the gates. Even when I showed them my accordion, brand new and shiny, told them my father's name and proclaimed kinship with the great kheleke, the security men refused to budge.

Why do you insist on seeing Khosi Mosotho Chakela? asked the one who looked arrogant and behaved like their boss. What poison are you bringing him?

How can I wish to kill the very man from whom I want mentorship? I asked. How can I wish to kill a Mosotho from my own area?

Who do you think kill our men of Lekhotla la Terene if not thugs from our own village?

Lekhotla la Terene – the Cult of the Train – was Khosi Mosotho Chakela's group of men who, clad in black-and-yellow blankets, sang his choruses known as makhele while he sang masholu, the singsong spoken-word hymns or lifela themselves. But the Men of the Cult of the Train did more than just sing. They were soldiers. The knobkerries that they wielded as part of their dance routine converted into weapons of war when things began to stink without being rotten. In addition to the semi-automatic rifles that suddenly appeared from arms caches whose location was known only to the leaders.

I stood at the gate displaying all the despondence I could muster.

You can see the Men of the Cult of the Train on Saturday evening if you go to Bochabela Hall, said another security guard who apparently felt sorry for me. If you are lucky you might see Khosi Mosotho Chakela himself there.

But his boss jumped in, hey uena monna, how do you know Ntate Chakela will be there?

And then he looked at me, shook his head, and said, Ntate Chakela is an old man and you people should let him rest. There is no way he will be performing there. The Cult of the Train has many eloquent men.

I gave up. I left for the township and found a good-time place, where for that whole night my accordion screeched popular songs of the townships rather than the hymns of the wanderers.

That Saturday I made a point of occupying a seat in the front row with the accordion on my lap. Though I had owned it for almost two weeks, my eyes were constantly drawn to its golden grille with the word Hohner running down the ornate embellishments, its pitch-black bellows, and its shimmering silver bass buttons and the white-and-black treble keyboard. I never even in my craziest dreams imagined that one day I would own such an instrument.

*

When Toloki left for Johannesburg he did not mention that he would return with such a big thing. All we knew was that he wanted to explore ways of crossing the big oceans to search for mourning in other cultures of the world. It was after he had mourned so powerfully that tourists who were passing by riding Basotho ponies stopped to witness and exclaimed that they had not known there was professional mourning in the culture of Basotho.

No, in the culture of Basotho there is no such thing as a professional mourner, he told them. It is something that I am introducing as a votary of my own Order of Professional Mourners. I am still its only member, or perhaps Noria is another one since she is both the love of my life and my manager. Indeed, even where we came from in the coastal city, there was never any such thing as professional mourning before me. It is something that I introduced. It is something that I invented.

The tourists found this fascinating.

I hate to tell you this, said one of them. Though you must have evolved your own style, you did not invent professional mourning.

They told him of various cultures, both in ancient history and in today's world, which had a tradition of mourners who were paid to mourn the deaths of strangers.

From that day Toloki spoke of nothing but going out in the world in search of mourning. Noria was quite excited about the idea. Together they would wander in Taiwan where they heard mourning was big business, in India where paid women known as Rudaali mourned the dead in the state of Rajasthan, in Spain where hired plañideras accompanied the funeral procession to the grave site wailing their hearts out. The thought of participating in these ceremonies and of exchanging ideas with these venerable professionals so excited the couple that Noria suggested that Toloki should go to Johannesburg and find out more about the costs and other things such as applying for visas. They didn't have passports either. Though these were necessary to enter Lesotho from South Africa, they had entered through what Basotho called the paqama gate – that is, using an illegal port of entry or just crossing the river that borders the two countries. Toloki would also investigate how they could obtain passports.

Noria wanted to go with Toloki, but he insisted that it would make the journey easier and lighter if he went alone.

*

Toloki had been gone for a week when the thing happened. Noria was sitting outside the mokhoro basking in the sun and moping. She had been keeping to herself since Toloki left. She must have missed him terribly. I brought her a bowl of salted likhobe – boiled maize kernels – that Moliehi had cooked the previous day. She asked me to join her when she saw me preparing to leave. I sat next to her on the bench.

Your sister will be mad at you for offering me this, said Noria.

No, I said. My sister is not a stingy person. Not about food, anyway.

I saw her cook these likhobe yesterday, but she only dished out for herself even though I was right there in the room with her.

That was very unlike Moliehi. Yet I didn't think Noria would lie about something like that.

I think she just wanted them to sleep before she shared them with us, I said. Likhobe are more delicious when you eat them the next day.

She didn't seem to buy it. Instead she looked me straight in the eye and asked, Why does your sister hate me so?

I don't think she hates you, I said.

What did I do to her? she insisted.

I thought you were now getting along.

I thought so too, she said. Remember when we came back from Puseletso Seema's feast? She seemed to have thawed towards me and Toloki. But suddenly she resumed her shit. Clearly, she does not want me here. I should have left with Toloki. We should have left for good.

Don't take her seriously, I said. She has her moods but means no harm.

She told me about her life with Toloki, from the time they were children, how she used to inspire Toloki's blacksmith father with her songs that made him create soaring figurines with various metals, how Toloki hated her because he thought she was a stuck-up bitch, and how after many years of taking different paths in life they got together and became lovers. I told her the story of the boy-child, he whose body would be meals for the vultures, but he who must be a kheleke of the world before that happened.

When the sun set and dusk crept in, we knew each other's stories, and there was softness between us. A measly slice of the moon rose like a sickle behind the hills. And we sat. Our mouths had dried of life-stories. Silence followed. Silence only from us, because frogs in the ponds continued to croak. And a lone owl hooted its unpleasant night song.

I noticed her hand was resting comfortably on my knee. As if it belonged there. I shifted a bit, trying hard not to alert her to my discomfort. When it gradually inched its way to places where dangerous things slept, I jumped up. This startled her.

You are not used to forward women? she asked with a mischievous lilt in her voice.

I was used to forward women, but they were a different kind of women. They were women of the good-time places. Of the timiti parties where my concertina tingled their veins like an aphrodisiac. Of the focho dances where they raised their legs high to display the spotlight – the chalk circle drawing attention to their jewels. Women who sang aggressive hymns that demeaned men into action. She was not a famo woman. She was Noria. Toloki's wife. Or lover. Or whatever they called each other.

You are afraid, aren't you? she said. A man like you who is a vagabond – leloabe – of the good-time places is scared to taste fruit that is standing right here in front of him saying come on, have a nibble?

Out of respect for Toloki, I stammered. She must not see that her words were wounding me. That was exactly what she was trying to do. Shame me to mindless desire. Demean me into action. The same tactic that famo women used. I dared not show any weakness. I dared not run away.

Leave Toloki out of this, she said. He is a good man, not a leloabe like you. A man is never hurt by transgressions he doesn't know about. Unless he hears of them from the transgressors. And then she added quickly in a hoarse whisper, I'm thirsty.

Likhobe can make you thirsty. Especially when they are liberally salted. I excused myself and returned with a bowl of sugared sour sorghum porridge – motoho. I took a small gulp and passed it to Noria. She shook her head and said, later in the night, maybe. It will not quench my present thirst.

A man is not told twice. A man is not asked twice either. Unless our elders were wrong in coining that idiom. Before I knew it, we were rolling in each other's arms on a moseme grass mat between bags of maize and beans. Darkness covered us like a blanket of shame.

Until the blinding light of a torch shone in Noria's eyes. In the midst of rhythmic groans and whines, neither of us had heard Moliehi pushing the door open. And she stood there behind the light, her body silhouetted by the measly moonlight framed by the door.

What manyala are you showing us under my father's roof? Moliehi screamed, calling what to us was mere mischief an abomination.

What business is it of yours, I screamed back as I reached for my pants on one of the sacks of produce. We are two adults doing adult things.

I pushed Moliehi out of the way and leapt out of the mokhoro as she continued to yell at Noria.

You have no shame? Is that what you remained here for? To do this bofebe – whoring – with my dirty brother?

Leave Toloki out of this, said Noria. What do you care about him?

I watched from the outside and was surprised how calm Noria was as Moliehi hit her with the light by brandishing the torch violently.

And with my brother too, said Moliehi, her voice so anguished you would have thought that of all the disgusting things in the world fornicating with me was the worst.

Your brother, not your husband, said Noria as calmly as ever. Unless you desire him too.

Moliehi screamed as if someone had stabbed her with a knife and said, It is true then that your mind is full of nothing but abomination.

49

She rushed out of the mokhoro. She passed me cowering by the door, waiting to rescue the rest of my clothes and said, Ntja tooe! You dog! She spat out the tooe so that I made no mistake: you dog in our language may mean the canine animal, and is therefore an insult when used for a human being. But it may also be a term of endearment for a man of great deeds, whether roguish or strait-laced. Tooe told me she meant this as an insult rather than a compliment.

The next morning, I threw my letlama blanket over my shoulder, took my concertina, and hit the road. I did not sing of Moliehi as I trod on pathways that led to the village of Matelile, though it was obligatory for a kheleke to boast of his sister's beauty and prowess. I sang about other things. I sang my heart out, the very songs I would sing at good-time places where my concertina would buy me enough beer to wet my parched throat and extinguish the wanton fires Noria had provoked.

For ten days I was soaked in hops. And in the seoeleoelele voices of dancing women hymn singers. And in the sublime stenches of sex. Every gyrating woman, either to my concertina or to my own gyrations, became Noria. Until the homing impulse was too strong to resist. I sang my way back home to Likhoele, hoping that Toloki would have returned and all transgressions would be the stuff of bad memories. We would all settle back to our normal anguished selves.

When I arrived the cocks were crowing the morning into being, and colours of dawn had silhouetted our three huts – the main one where Moliehi, child of my mother, slept, the middle one where I slept and cooking was done in winter, and the mokhoro where Toloki and Noria slept among bags of sorghum, maize and beans.

Moliehi would be awake at that time. She woke up at the same time as fowls in the chicken run. I went to the main hut to tell her

I was back. I didn't expect her to welcome me with a hug, especially because since I had found Toloki and Noria at Famole's funeral and brought them home with me, I had not been away for so many days. She even thought I had been cured of my wanderlust, which she called boloabe – vagabondry – and soon I would be a responsible working miner, then a husband, and then the crowning glory: a father. Nevertheless, I was home; she was bound to sigh with relief.

Moliehi, child of my mother, I said as I opened the door and entered. Even in the dim light I could see two entwined bodies in bed mapped out by the blanket. I chuckled because in all the years I had known Moliehi, which means since she was born as I was the older brother though she liked to mother me, I had never known her to have a lover. Often I teased her that I would die before eating her bohali cattle since she was not showing any interest in men. Perhaps this was what she did when I was away – sneaking men into her bed. This was my time to annoy her. And embarrass her and her lover.

Molotsana tooe! I said, laughing, calling her a sneaky person. So, you bring men home when I am not here?

Men? What men? she asked.

At the same time Noria raised her head from the pillow.

I did not know what had happened in my absence to bring these two together, but after that they became as close as saliva is to the tongue. I noticed that Noria no longer slept in the mokhoro but spent her nights and most of the day in the main hut. This continued for days. For weeks.

Even when Toloki returned Noria did not seem to welcome him back with any enthusiasm.

Toloki, standing like a magician who was about to perform the most amazing trick, announced that he had a surprise for each one of us. We all looked at the big box in front of him expectantly.

For Noria, he said, brandishing two passports, I give you the world. I managed to bribe Home Affairs people in Johannesburg for these. All we need now are visas, which we can get in Maseru. These cost me quite a bundle, but they are worth every cent. Now we can travel the world to learn new ways of mourning.

Noria was stone-faced. Moliehi was wide-eyed.

I thought you would be happy, said Toloki. It is what we said we would do after learning of all the cultures that pride themselves on professional mourning.

Noria did not respond. She looked shell-shocked.

And for you, boy-child, he whose body shall be food for the vultures, I give you the gift of song, he said as he took out a shimmering German-style Hohner accordion.

I was as shell-shocked as Noria, but for different reasons. No man had ever done anything like that for me. And this was a man I had betrayed.

You took us in, boy-child, and gave us a home, though we were total strangers to you. You joined me in my mourning with your hallowed concertina. Before we cross the seas, boy-child, we'll try your new accordion at a funeral.

The two women were still stone-faced. I suspected that Moliehi, child of my mother, worried that with an accordion my boloabe would be worse. But she didn't say anything. She just stared at Toloki. I stared at him too, expecting him to announce the third surprise.

There is nothing more, said Toloki. Your sister's gift is that finally we are leaving her in peace. She clearly did not want us here. We apologise for being a burden.

I was offended, and I told him so. He might have bought me an accordion, but I didn't think he should be so ungracious to my sister.

Toloki is right, child of my mother, said Moliehi calmly. I do not expect him to give me a gift other than the one I already have.

Moliehi abruptly left the main hut. Noria followed. But before she exited, she turned to Toloki and whispered, I do not want to leave, Toloki. Maybe you should go on your own in search of mourning. You are the professional mourner.

Toloki was taken aback. He stood there for a while as if he didn't know what to do next. And then he burst out, Can you believe this? She sent me to Johannesburg to find out ways of going overseas in search of mourning. I return with more than an accomplished mission – with passports! Does she show appreciation? No! She is no longer interested!

Soon the two women were making a fire under a three-legged cast-iron pot preparing to cook the meal of the day in front of the mokhoro. And I was sitting on a rock near the corral trying my new accordion. It was unwieldy and its notes were more complex than those of my concertina. But I was going to master it.

My accordion. The days that followed I was either playing it or just admiring it. Even when the bellows were stationary and the accordion was silent, my fingers found comfort in tickling the buttons and the keys in some imagined tune.

*

I was doing exactly that as I sat in the front row in Bochabela Hall with the accordion resting on my lap. The Men of the Cult of the Train were singing manngae – songs of the traditional initiation-school graduands – and were marching rhythmically from one end of the stage to the other, their ornamented sticks raised, their black-and-white shoes shimmering, and their black-and-yellow blankets spotlessly new. They were singing a cappella but my fingers insisted on accompanying their song with a mean accordion that only I could hear.

A group of much younger men, most of them young enough to be called boys, but men nonetheless because they were all circumcised at an initiation school, entered and by the sheer force of their numbers pushed the previous group to the back and the sides. They were not confined only to the stage but occupied the whole area in front of our seats. I could smell their armpits and see sweat maps under their arms as they were not wearing blankets but black-and-gold T-shirts emblazoned *Ha e Tlale Terene*, which translates to Let the Train be Full. This may also translate to The Train is Never Full, depending on your tone and emphasis on some syllables. There were more letters filling the whole T-shirt both in front and at the back. Because of their movement I struggled to read, but I was keen to know what the message was. Ultimately, I pieced it together: *Bolokanang Sechaba sa Khosi*. Look After One Another Khosi's Nation. *Ha Re Bolokeng Khotso*. Let Us Preserve the Peace. They were all carrying sticks that were pointing to the ceiling.

They sang a chorus in the makhele style, their voices clean and innocent. The song was titled 'Ke Hana Ke Holile', and it was about Khosi Mosotho Chakela himself, reputed to be now aged.

Even though I'm old like this, when the sounds of war roar I hobble along and join the people. Though I have aged like this, the old man that I am, when the train is full, I stumble aboard and go to the people.

By the people I took it he meant his fighters.

Three old men hobbled along in a slow dance, and one of them suddenly beat the raised sticks of the young men with great aggression, creating an ominous rhythm. This was the kalla dance, which was mock stick fighting. The young men held tight to their sticks and did not respond to the old man's faux violence. One of the young men screamed repeatedly in a woman's soprano.

A man with a blazing accordion entered from one end of the stage performing a frenzied dance. Another one entered from the other end playing drums made of a tin fuel container and a rubber drumhead. The chorus of the boys and the accordion made for a stirring combination.

Now you will see real excitement, said a man sitting next to me.

He didn't need to tell me that; excitement was already pulsating through the hall.

The accordion man is Mohalalitoe and the drum man is Mochini-oa-Ipommpa, said the man next to me, as if he was introducing me to his old friends. Of course, I had heard of the names, though I had never seen them in action in the flesh. I had seen Mohalalitoe on television once when I was at the camp in Mafeteng. Here he was much closer, and his face was ragged like that of a man who had been battered by many rains.

At that point the man himself entered. Khosi Mosotho Chakela! His face was round like that of a well-fed baby and was beaming with friendliness. Yet he was dancing a dance of an aged man, hunched shoulders, walking stick and all. After all, the song was a lamentation of the warrior's old age. He did not look old at all, unless you want to tell me that fifty is aged. His hair did not show the slightest trace of grey. He was a roly-poly man in a brown coat with a fur collar and a beer belly that defied gravity. He danced in an exaggerated gait, now and then pretending to fall, and then spinning around to display his agility.

The chorus gave way and only the accordion and drum remained. He sang his lifela, while the three authentic greybeards danced next to him, but making sure they did not steal his thunder.

When I am old like this, I become a man of great intellect, declaimed Chakela in the sing-song voice of the hymns of the wanderers. When I age, I become sharp-minded and eagle eyed. You will only see with the hanging flesh that, hey, this thing is old. But my eloquence will not age, will not end, my warrior spirit lives forever, oeeele-oelele. When the war is fought you will not believe I am an old man.

He continued his faux arthritic dance to the cheers and applause of the audience.

The man was masterful in every way I wished I could be. In the ease of his dance, his command of the stage, his lovable demeanour. My heart was pumping faster and faster, and my breathing was laboured. My fingers rebelled! They refused to be tamed any more. They became ungovernable.

My throbbing head told me some of that applause was rightfully mine. Khosi Mosotho Chakela had no right to hog it all to himself. The people shall share. At least that's what my fingers twitched. Especially those of the left hand. Without further warning all of them, except for the thumb, pressed hard on the buttons and a resounding bass filled the hall, backing Mohalalitoe's accordion with new notes that complicated his song. He was startled.

The hall broke into thunderous applause and cheers and whistles. They must have thought I was part of the act. Chakela, an old pro, did not evince any surprise. Did not even wince. Instead he danced his way to the exit while Mohalalitoe and Mochini-oa-Ipommpa continued to play with gusto in keeping with the cheers. Perhaps hoping to drown my accordion. I was up on my feet by that time, complicating the music even further, not only with bass buttons but with treble notes as well. The dexterity of my fingers left even me open-mouthed and them wide-eyed.

Mohalalitoe, which by the way means arum-lily – don't ask me how such an ugly weather-beaten man who looked like he didn't have a friendly relationship with water was named after a water plant with lovely flowers – led his drummer and the makhele chorus boys to the exit. I remained standing and playing. The crowds gathered around me and moved to my beats. When I broke into a hymn the crowd went berserk.

Later that evening I was in a Mercedes-Benz sitting at the back between two unsmiling men. Their boss wanted to see me, they said. They had patiently waited for me at the door while I basked in the adulation of the fans of the Cult of the Train. I was happy that finally I was going to meet Khosi Mosotho Chakela face to face.

It was not to be. At a house in Heidedal, formerly a coloureds-only township during apartheid, I was confronted by Mohalalitoe and Mochini-oa-Ipommpa. They were still in their black-and-yellow blankets and were glaring down at me.

Are you now done with hijacking our event? asked Mohalalitoe.

I didn't go there to hijack your concert, bo-ntate, I pleaded. I only wanted to meet my hero, Khosi Mosotho Chakela.

Why? asked Mochini.

He looks like an assassin, said Mohalalitoe. They sent him to kill our Morena.

I was surprised that they called Chakela a chief. I knew his village, Matelile Ha Makhakhe, and he was not a chief there. Perhaps they gave him the title of Morena because he is the boss of his own Cult of the Train. Perhaps Khosi, which also means chief, is not a name but his title.

Who sent you? insisted Mochini.

No one. I want to be a member of the Cult of the Train. I want to be mentored by the great Khosi Mosotho Chakela.

Do you think people just join Lekhotla la Terene as if it's a political party? asked Mohalalitoe.

I thought the great master would see my talent and would allow me to join, I said. I so very much want to play with him and learn greatness from him.

Both men found this funny and laughed. I was offended.

You think I'm not good enough? I asked, not attempting to hide my annoyance.

Who deceived you that you're good enough? asked Mochini.

Of course he is, Mochini-oa-Ipommpa. We both know that, said Mohalalitoe. We have just seen that he knows how to work the crowd.

He is very irritating, said Mochini. I don't like him.

Mohalalitoe seemed to enjoy Mochini's annoyance. That gave me courage to defend myself against him.

I would not like myself either if all I did in life was play a car-tyre drum, I said glaring at him as if I was challenging him to a fight.

Take it easy, boys, said Mohalalitoe laughing his head off.

Mochini-oa-Ipommpa stood up from the sofa and walked out in a huff. But not before spitting out that I was talking shit. Mohalalitoe turned to look at me and was serious once again.

To which mophato do you belong? he asked.

Mophato could be the residence of initiates at an initiation school. Or the school itself. I shook my head because I had never been to one. I was brought up by Christian converts who did not believe in the old traditions of Basotho people.

Don't tell me you are not circumcised; that you do not know koma, the secret song of the mountain?

I shook my head once more. I did not understand what a circumcised penis would have to do with my ambition to be part of the Cult of the Train.

You saw all those men singing makhele choruses, the men of Lekhotla la Terene? There are many of them, as you saw, but they are one. Ke bana ba monna. They are children of a man. They speak with one voice. They will die for one another. Do you know where they learned that unity from? That loyalty? That dedication? From mophato. From the circumcision school. They don't only cut foreskins there. They mould boys into one man, the man who would die for Lekhotla la Terene. Khosi Mosotho Chakela would never trust you or your loyalty if you have not gone through the same circumcision school or if you are not a product of the same mesuoe and lingaka – teachers and doctors. You would be an outsider in the Cult of the Train.

My heart sank. I would do anything to be part of this group. Even go through circumcision though I am old enough to be a father to some of those boys. If the road to Chakela's group was only through a particular initiation mophato, it would be the same with the other rival groups as well. The oath of loyalty one took to the leading lifela singer and accordionist was closely linked to the secrets of the mountain. It meant that if I didn't go for circumcision and initiation I would never be accepted in any group as a kheleke – the eloquent one.

*

Back at Likhoele I mulled over initiation into manhood and circumcision. I was a grown man and resented that I had to go through an institution to be deemed a man. No one ever doubted my manhood before. I was an accomplished musician and I resented that I had to go through the ritual of chopping off my foreskin in order to be counted among the greats. But what choice did I have? I resolved that next winter, when the boys went to the mountain, I would have no choice but to follow them. I would go to Matelile and find out which mophato was sponsored by the Cult of the Train and join.

The accordion helped my ruminations. I spent the whole day sitting on a rock by my father's cattle corral playing softly to myself. Sometimes Toloki came and tried to keep me company. But I was not up to any conversation. He came and sat and listened. At the slightest pause he jumped in and asked what had caused my sadness. I said nothing. I didn't confess my plans to go for circumcision. He said no man sat alone all day shunning even food and playing koliamalla – lamentations – as if someone had died. I said it was only my spirit that had died. Or was in the process of dying. And then played furiously to shut him up. He stood up and left.

He resorted to standing outside my door early in the morning, waiting to catch me before I got to the corral. He walked with me, pleading that we needed to talk. Things were not going well for him and Noria. She preferred to spend most of her time with Moliehi, child of my mother. They sat together all day long, they cooked together, they walked together to gather firewood and cow dung. They walked hand in hand, giggling like teenagers. At night Noria preferred to sleep in the main hut where Moliehi slept. When he had put his foot down that she should spend the night with him in the mokhoro, she moped for the whole night and did not respond when he touched her. When he tried to force himself on her, she closed her thighs tightly and elbowed him away. Therefore, nothing happened between them.

Your sister has given the love of my life medicine to hate me, said Toloki.

Why would she do anything like that? I said. Moliehi is not a witch. They bonded when you were away and became friends. That's all there is to it.

60

She has even lost interest in my mourning, said Toloki. I can't mourn without Noria.

You told me you were a mourner long before you rediscovered each other at her son's funeral.

Oh yes, we rediscovered each other at a funeral where I was mourning. And then we walked this long road together. I come from very far with that woman. Your sister cannot come between us. She must not come between you and me either. We made a wonderful team mourning together. We should continue to do so.

I promised him that should any mourning gig present itself I would certainly join him. After all, the man bought me an accordion. And the guilt hit me once more: I hoped he never got to hear that I did naughty things with his woman. Joining him for some mourning sessions was the least I could do for him. It was the least I could do for myself too. If I was not going to be a man of the Cult of the Train, perhaps my destiny was to mourn the dead.

That afternoon I saw Moliehi approaching my rock and I was filled with dread. She was bound to find something to chastise me for. Maybe that I was not eating enough; I must not come crying to her if I died of starvation. Or that Toloki must have bought me this accordion only to annoy her. Or that I was a lazy bum who sat by the corral playing the accordion when other men were digging gold from the intestines of the earth or were becoming great farmers – lihoai – on their fathers' fields. Or anything else motherly. She should have married a good man and mothered her own children instead of mothering an older brother.

Even before she reached me, she smiled. I became even more uneasy. She smiled effortlessly now, ever since she bonded with Noria. She even laughed. I had heard them laugh into the night in the main hut.

What is eating you, child of my mother? she asked, giggling.

This giggling thing that you do lately doesn't suit you, I said.

You hate happiness? she asked.

For you, yes. Since when have you become a happy person?

She sat down on the rock Toloki had used the other day.

I have a plan, she said.

And then laid it out. Now that I had such a shimmering accordion, I could be a star. No, not of the timiti or famo or focho. Not the leloabe I was when I was a concertina man. Not a vagabond. Not even a molelere wanderer. A star who appeared on South African television in the *Roots* programme that showcased traditional and indigenous music at 5:30 in the afternoon on Saturdays. She and Noria wanted to dance for me. I would play the accordion and sing lifela while they danced in the background as they saw women do in most of the videos on the programme. Every musician worth anything at all had dancing women in the background.

You want to be a dancing woman? You who said music has turned me into a leloabe, I asked, laughing. I thought she was joking.

Noria made me change my mind, said Moliehi.

In that case, Noria is a bad influence. Your friendship with her is up to no good, I said. I don't like it that you spend all the time with her, separating her from her husband.

They are not really married, she said.

It doesn't matter. You are not going to be my dancer. You're not going to be anyone's dancer.

Why not?

Because I have seen how women dancers are used by men, I said with finality and I stood up to leave.

She followed me as I walked towards my hut.

How do you know they are being used by those men? How do you know they are not using those men? Who is using who?

Is that from Noria too? I asked as I entered my hut and slammed the door shut.

It must be from Noria. She's a bad influence. Moliehi had never wanted to be a focho dancer. She despised both the dances and the way of life. She despised me for being an itinerant musician who played that kind of music. The music of maloabe, as she called it. And now she wanted to be a focho dancer?

I stormed out of the hut and went looking for Toloki. I could see Moliehi and Noria at the pumpkin patch cutting pumpkin leaves to cook as vegetables. They looked at me and giggled like naughty schoolgirls.

Toloki was sitting on a bench outside the mokhoro looking miserable.

I beg you, I said softly, just talk to your woman to stop influencing my sister to change from what she has always been.

It is your sister, man! Toloki yelled. It is your sister who is busy influencing the love of my life to change from who she has always been. I come from very far with Noria and look what is now happening.

It can't be Moliehi, I said. She has been a good person all along.

Do you know that ever since I returned from Johannesburg, I do not know anything about moseme? Completely!

Toloki's face was melting as if he was going to cry. I knew what he was talking about when he mentioned moseme, the grass mat on which we slept when using the floor instead of a bed. He was talking about sex, and it always embarrassed me to hear about other people's sexual life or lack thereof. I told him the issues of moseme were really none of my business.

Why don't you talk to your woman about it? I suggested. Find out what the problem is? Find out what wrong you did to her? Perhaps you did something wrong and you are not aware of it.

Do I look like I didn't talk with her about it? Of course, I have talked with her. She always says there is nothing wrong, and yet continues to refuse to sleep in the hut that you lent us. Now every damn night she sleeps in the main hut. She is with your sister day and night. I think your sister is trying to punish me. She hated me from the very first day you brought us here. Please ask her to leave Noria alone. We'll leave. We'll go far away from here.

A Range Rover stopped near the corral and two men walked towards the main hut. I recognised them immediately. Mohalalitoe and Mochini-oa-Ipommpa.

Ke mona baholoane. I am here, my elder brothers, I called as I stood up to meet them.

My heart was skipping some beats. They must have been sent by Khosi Mosotho Chakela. He must have been impressed by my playing when I inadvertently hijacked his concert. Surely, he wanted me to join the Cult of the Train even though I was not from any initiation school. Unless he sent them to kill me.

The women, with basins full of pumpkin leaves and a few unripe green pumpkins, came closer to satisfy their curiosity.

Mohalalitoe's greeting was brief and was not accompanied by the traditional banter of enquiring about the health of the household, the rains that were stubborn and were refusing to fall, the colds from which the family was suffering and the deaths that were stalking the land. None of those niceties. And that made Moliehi suspect that they were not on a friendly mission.

What do they want? she asked. And, turning to me, What did you do?

We want him, said Mochini, who also had been quite miserly with the greeting.

Please come with us to the camp of Mafeteng, said Mohalalitoe. We have some business to talk with you.

My friend must come with me, I said, pointing at Toloki.

Mohalalitoe shook his head and said, It is a private matter. Very private.

Ke banna ba Lekhotla la Terene, I said, addressing myself to Moliehi to assure her I was in safe hands. These are Men of the Cult of the Train. These are Khosi Mosotho Chakela's men.

Though Moliehi was protesting, I got into the car with them. Without my accordion. Without my ornamented stick. They said I would not need them where we were going.

Chakela would never want you as his protégé, said Mohalalitoe, as he negotiated the dirt road out of the village.

Then what do you want with me? I asked.

The Cult of the Train does not want maqai like you, he added with uncalled-for glee.

Maqai is not a nice word. It is what circumcised men disparagingly call uncircumcised ones. I did not respond, though my chest was filling up with fury. Did these men fetch me from my father's house where I was minding my own business to insult me?

I do not play my accordion with my penis, I burst out finally, after a long pause. Whether it is circumcised or not, it makes no difference; my fingers can press the buttons and the keys until the accordion screams like an orgasmic woman.

They burst out laughing.

I like him, said Mochini. He's full of shit but I like him.

I saw him that day in Bloemfontein, said Mohalalitoe. He's not only full of shit. He's a wizard at the accordion. He knows how to work a crowd. He's the right fit for our outfit.

They were exchanging these words between themselves on the front seats, but I butted in. After all, I was the subject of their praise. I hid my excitement though. They had already proclaimed that I was full of shit. I couldn't afford to spoil my new-found reputation.

65

Right fit? Does it mean I'll be joining the Cult of the Train?

No, said Mohalalitoe. Khosi Mosotho Chakela does not even know we are here.

He would cut our balls off if he knew we were here, said Mochini-oa-Ipommpa, laughing at what he thought was a brilliant joke. He was becoming more relaxed around me. Hopefully the grudge he held against me for calling him a mere player of car-tyre drums was dissipating.

Then why am I here? I asked. Where are you taking me?

It is a long story, said Mohalalitoe.

He told me the story and it wasn't long at all. They were rene-gades, intending to break away from the Cult of the Train to form their own group. They were here to recruit me to join them, even though I did not come through the right channels, namely a mo-phato.

At the initiation school, boys are moulded into men and are taught the values of loyalty, said Mohalalitoe. When you have recruited your followers from there, they are bound to be faithful to you for the rest of their lives.

You came from a mophato yourselves, didn't you? How come you are now betraying Chakela? What happened to the values you learned there and the oath you took? I asked.

I told you it was risky to recruit this man, said Mochini. You hear now the questions he's asking?

It is a simple question, Mochini, said Mohalalitoe. Once we were boys and our loyalty was unquestioning. Then we matured into men with families and responsibilities and realised that we were not being treated fairly. It's all about money. It's all about the limelight. We are tired of being in the background.

So, you want me to be in your background? I asked.

Oh no, you will be the lead accordionist, said Mohalalitoe. You'll be the main singer of the hymns. We'll all run the business like equal partners. But when it comes to war, I'll be the commander. And when it comes to mining, Mochini will be the commander.

What we'll be doing here goes against the grain, added Mochini. Normally the lead accordionist and hymn singer is also the commander of war and of mining operations.

The bit about mining confused me. But I did not question it at the time. I was just mesmerised by the fact that these men, hardened and experienced in the ways of the famo music business, were offering me stardom.

Mohalalitoe confessed that things were not as rosy as they used to be at the Cult of the Train. Money was becoming tight because of the competition from other famo groups – especially an outfit called Letlama, named both after a regiment of King Moshoeshoe I two hundred years ago and a famous brand of blankets much beloved by Basotho fuckboys.

I knew of Letlama very well because it was composed of men from Thabana Morena, one of the villages in the Accordion Triangle, which was also the home of Khosi Mosotho Chakela and the late Famole. Letlama's influence and membership, however, later spread throughout the district of Mafeteng.

The group was reputed to have the best musicians. Three of those whose hymns sent me reeling were Lekase, Mahlanya and Lisuoa.

Letlama rose rapidly, taking the whole of South Africa by storm.

War had to break out between the Men of the Train and Letlama, and Mohalalitoe distinguished himself with his brutality. The Train people eliminated a lot of the Letlama people. The latter were badly treated, and they began to organise and arm themselves with illegal guns. They became the most brutal gangsters among all the musicians. They were known to hide their AK-47 and R4 rifles under their Letlama blankets and to draw them at the slightest irritation. Even the Cult of the Train was wary of provoking them into war again. Each group kept to its turf, mostly abandoned gold mines in the various provinces of South Africa.

Letlama's power was slightly weakened when it broke into two rival factions: Letlama le Letšo – the Black Letlama – and Letlama le Lekhubelu – the Red Letlama. The blankets they wore were of those colours. The great musician, Lekase, which means Coffin, led the main Letlama that distinguished itself with black blankets. His music was reputed to be the best in terms of quality.

I knew Lekase from our youth, said Mohalalitoe. We went to the same mophato. Though one of the greatest MaRussia I have known, he was not a man of war during those days. At least not against his fellow musicians. War was forced on him by us, the generals of the Cult of the Train. What do you do when you're constantly attacked, and you've never been a coward? But now his young followers, fresh from initiation schools, are the deadliest.

That's what our elders meant when they warned us never to provoke a snake in its hole, added Mochini.

I was keen to hear more of the musicians and their cliques from these insiders, especially the aspect about the gold mines, but we had arrived in the camp of Mafeteng. And by the way, when we talk of a camp here, we really mean a town. The district capital towns of Lesotho were called camps because during the various wars they were either dominated by, or began their lives as, camps and forts of British garrisons.

We arrived at a police station and headed for one of the houses. In the nomenclature of Lesotho, a police station was the area where houses and barracks of the police were located rather than an office of a local police force. That was called a charge office.

Before he knocked at the door Mohalalitoe asked, Are you with us or not?

Do I look like a fool to you? I asked. Of course, I am with you.

Don't do any shit on us, said Mochini. Mohalalitoe may like you, but we'll have no choice but to kill you.

He means if you betray us, said Mohalalitoe. But I know you won't. You are too hungry for fame to betray us. And you know that you can't get it from the Cult of the Train. It is a closed shop.

Like I said, do I look like a fool to you?

It turned out we were at the house of the Deputy District Police Commissioner, Tom-Tom Seabo. He welcomed us like old friends and served us beer in his living room crowded with sofas, display cabinets, room dividers, hi-fi sets and a big-screen television. Apparently he had been watching a soccer game, and the volume was high. He didn't try to lower it as he and Mohalalitoe conferred while Mochini and I pretended to be engrossed in the soccer.

They say the ear is a thief.

Oh no, I heard Mohalalitoe tell the policeman, the district commissioner will never know you are working for our side. No one will talk about it. Just like she didn't tell you that she is on the payroll of the Cult of the Train. We know how to keep secrets because our lives are at stake if anything slips out.

I saw Mohalalitoe hand a fat white envelope to the deputy commissioner. The man was going to protect the new group from the long arm of the law and from other factions. If any of the members were to be charged, the deputy commissioner would make the docket disappear.

Thus, I saw with my own eyes that it was not just hot air when MaRussia boasted that, unlike the old days when their bosses were on the payroll of the police, today's MaRussia were able to buy and own the police.

4

The scent of the arum-lily

I have always loved and trusted you, Men of the Cult of the Train. I have traversed valleys with you. I am ruled by the big society of men. The Cult of the Train. Though I am your leader, you are my rulers. I am a servant leader, a commoner king. I am ruled by real men. Warrior men. Not some little brats of boys. Sirs, fathers, board the train. Let the train be full so that we leave. Let the train depart from the station.

At this point the kheleke transformed 'Haesale', as the piece was titled, from a song to a hymn. The accordion and the drums, likewise, became more intense. My eyes were agog as if a strong magnet was pulling the physical eyeballs themselves to the television screen. My head was swaying left to right to the fast-paced dances of the men blanketed in black and yellow.

Mme Mpuse looked at me, shook her head, took a bite of a ginger biscuit and a sip of tea. I disregarded her. I could not pretend I was not impressed by the performance of Khosi Mosotho Chakela on the television screen.

Haesale ke le rata ke le tšepa banna ba Terene. I have always loved and trusted you, Men of the Train. I have crossed expansive wastelands with you. In difficulties, in hard times. I became your chief because a chief is made a chief by his people. A chief cannot be a chief without his people. Even I, a leader, Khosi, a chief, I am ruled by this society of men. It is a great society of real men, not roguish boys. Where there is no leadership there is no youth and no elder. A place where even a rat can lead. We of the Cult of the Train respect a pact. Partnership is respected and honoured. So is leadership. It is a law that was written down and passed. We pledged ourselves to this organisation. We have sworn our loyalty to it. The Cult of the Train. We are like nuns who have bound themselves to the Roman Catholic Church. I swear by my grandmother who died a painful death. Dear Grandma, even where you are sleeping, you are the god of my ancestors, because you are the one who is protecting me, my parent.

It is an ominous song, said Maleshoane, the ample woman sitting next to me. She was the lead dancer in Mme Mpuse's troupe, and her eyes were glued to the television screen just like mine. She looked at me for confirmation. I looked at Mme Mpuse for confirmation. She was non-committal. She pretended to be disinterested. Perhaps uninterested. Bored. I knew it was pretence because at some stage I furtively observed her body twitching to the rhythm despite herself.

The hymn singer then went into the praises of his sister, Pontšo, as was the custom with hymns of the wayfarers, and paid tribute to his village and its people. He ended by citing day-to-day events that were so mundane they might be known only to him and those from his village.

It was an ominous song. Maleshoane was right. I did not say that to the two women sitting with me in the lounge of the Victoria Hotel in Maseru. I said it to myself.

Another group was playing. The accordionist was so tiny it looked like the bellows were going to swallow him. Maleshoane giggled. Mme Mpuse continued with her indifference. The music was good, nonetheless. Nothing ominous about this one. Quite joyful actually. Something about herdboys and the tricks they were apt to play when they were supposed to be looking after cattle at the meraka cattle posts. The kind of music I would like to be known for rather than the warlike songs of rival hymn singers.

But the ominous song continued to ring in my head. Not because of its infectious melody. But the words. I knew to whom they were directed. The rebels. Those who thought they could break away from the Cult of the Train without repercussions. Those who either betrayed the oath or were planning to. Mohalalitoe and men of his ilk. Mohalalitoe and Mochini-oa-Ipommpa, both of whom were in hiding, claiming in their messages to me that some hotheads from the Train were gunning for them, and assuring me that I should stay calm as no one was after me. I was never part of the Cult of the Train in any event, so they would have no reason to spoil my day by killing me.

I did not know when the song was recorded, or when the music video was made. It could have been an old recording for all I cared. But it spoke to the present: the actions of Mohalalitoe and his drummer sidekick. The message was clear: to break ranks with your comrades would have an unhappy ending. It didn't say so in so many words. But I could read between the lines. Even Shoane – an endearment for Maleshoane I gave myself permission to use the previous night – could read between the lines. She was the first to observe it was an ominous song, though she didn't even know about Mohalalitoe and Mochini-oa-Ipommpa.

It was cold outside the Cult of the Train once you had been inside. Only those who were never inside in the first place had no conception of that chill.

I shifted a bit to make more room for Shoane whose heaving breasts, abundant thighs and hanging love-handles – all mapped out conspicuously by her orange seshoeshoe dress – were overflowing on the two-seater sofa.

I am a lot of person, she said with a mischievous twinkle.

You are fine, I said.

Of course I am fine. I don't need anyone's opinion on that.

She was fine all right. She had a very attractive face, very smooth skin with a natural glow. It was spoiled only by a blonde wig that sat like an orphan on her head, not even attempting to hide her finely plaited black hair. It served more the function of a hat than of faux hair.

You could have been fine with me last night, I said, talking softly, closer to her ear. I still don't understand why you said no.

She elbowed me.

Shhh ... you want Mme Mpuse to hear of your dirty mind?

Mme Mpuse heard of my dirty mind. After all, her easy chair was one of the two flanking the two-seater. She shook her head pityingly.

I am old, you children, she said, I have had my day. What makes you think I care about your botekatse?

She called my attempt at courtship whoring. I didn't see it that way. I genuinely wanted to cultivate some relationship with Maleshoane.

I saw her for the first time the previous morning when I arrived at the Victoria Hotel from Likhoele and was whisked into the hall where Mme Mpuse, a drummer and four dancers, all women, were rehearsing. She was one of the four, and she attracted my immediate attention because of her stage presence.

Even as I played the accordion backing Mme Mpuse's songs and hymns, my eyes kept on stealing to the dancers. My eyes were supposed to focus on the singer. They were supposed to dance with her movements, and smile whenever she said something clever or humorous. My whole face was supposed to beam only at Mme Mpuse. But Maleshoane's self-assured dance kept on messing up my attention. At one point Mme Mpuse stopped the hymn in mid-sentence and glared at me.

Your heart is not in my song, Moliehi's brother, she said. Your heart is pumping in your penis instead.

She was right. Instead of paying attention to the words of her hymns and their meaning, and then responding accordingly with the music, I was daydreaming of being swallowed by Maleshoane's body and then sinking deeper and deeper into an abyss.

I felt very bad. The rehearsal was becoming a disaster.

Mme Mpuse had sent a message all the way to Likhoele that I join her with my accordion. She emphasised that it was a one-performance-only gig, and I should not expect anything beyond that. Her regular band, Tau ea Linare, was doing some work in South Africa.

Her invitation, though unexpected, came at the right time when Mohalalitoe and Mochini were lying low, waiting for the dust to settle. But it also came at the wrong time because I had a funeral engagement with Toloki. A big funeral. A funeral of an important musician who had been assassinated by a rival gang at an illegal gold mine in Gauteng. The bereaved wanted Toloki to grace the funeral with his atrocious mourns and boy-child's accordion. I had agreed to mourn with him with my accordion and concertina. That suggestion had excited him greatly. I would play the accordion when we needed some churchy ambience, and then the concertina for those high-pitched moments when he sounded like mating cats.

Toloki hoped to recapture Noria's heart with the most heart-rending acts of mourning ever seen. They had been brought together by mourning at the coastal city after they had parted in their childhood village for many years. Their reunion had been at the funeral of her son, Vutha, who had been murdered in the political upheavals of the time. He was a professional mourner at Vutha's funeral. That was where they rediscovered each other.

Toloki was very much moved when he narrated these events. He hoped his mourning at this funeral of a great musician would impress Noria so much she would love him again.

What makes you think she does not love you any more? I asked.

She is under a bad influence, said Toloki. She is with your sister more than ever before. Sometimes days pass without seeing her at all. Not the slightest glimpse of her.

And then the bombshell! I was not going to perform with him because I had been invited to back Mme Mpuse in Maseru. That really broke him. I saw him staring at my accordion and shaking his head wistfully. Maybe he was cursing himself for ever buying it for me.

I couldn't have said no to Mme Mpuse. It was a break I had been yearning for – to play once more with this kheleke. To establish my name so that one day they could point at me and say, you see that kheleke, that boy-child who will be torn apart by vultures one day, yes, Moliehi's brother himself, you see him, he once played with Puseletso Seema.

You might remember that I had begged her once to let me play with her. To mentor me even.

And the first opportunity she gave me I got distracted by a dancing woman! You might say it was a second opportunity because I once played with her at the camp of Mafeteng. But it was a small do and I was still a concertina boy in those days. The first opportunity as a mature man of the accordion. The first opportunity after I had begged her.

I tried to redeem myself at the Victoria Hotel Poolside, a venue famous in Lesotho for its parties and performances by some of the top bands and DJs in the country and from South Africa.

Mme Mpuse looked like a chubby miner in white overalls and gumboots. Instead of a miner's hardhat she wore a red beanie. I followed her as she sang and danced near the edge of the swimming pool, my accordion backing her simple song with a beat that was sending the crowd on the lawn into a dancing fever. Boys and girls, most with cans of beer, doing the Sesotho dances they had seen on television being performed by male and female famo dancers. The same dances our four dancing women were performing in the area designated the stage near the palisade fence. The drummer next to the women kept up the rhythm, fuelling my accordion into a staccato that turned the dances into bedroom movements.

The song, however, had nothing to do with the bedroom. The lyrics were urging the people to stop overgrazing. Let the horses come so that we ride and leave. So that we ride to the cattle posts. All the cows and their calves. Protect the pastures so that you can raise cattle that are fat and beautiful.

I do not know if drunken revellers ever listen to the words. I don't think they cared one bit what the song was about. Horses, cattle, pastures; under bright lights at a poolside party, it didn't matter. It was enough that the beat sent them to a dance nirvana.

The audience broke into cheers and whistles. Some of them stopped dancing and applauded. It was not for Mme Mpuse or me. It was for Maleshoane. She was performing a clownish focho dance. I was amazed at her agility despite her carriage.

All the world loves a fat dancer.

Mme Mpuse sang only the song and didn't get into the hymn part. I had heard the hymn on radio before and I had been wondering how she was going to handle the dramatic dialogue between herself and another kheleke about boys who had set the pastures on fire since we had not rehearsed it during the day. She saved the night by omitting it.

After the show Mme Mpuse said to me, one day you'll be a sought-after kheleke. But never be led by your penis. That's what has destroyed great men. Be led by the music.

Later that night I found the women in the bar huddled together at one table. I didn't spot them at first and then I heard, there's Moliehi's brother.

None of these women were from Likhoele; obviously, they didn't know Moliehi. That told me they knew her name from some of my hymns. I had no recording of any hymn yet. Therefore, they must have heard them, or of them, at some of the good-time places in the villages in the Accordion Triangle. I had forgotten that during the rehearsal Mme Mpuse had addressed me as Moliehi's brother.

I joined them. Maleshoane was the only one drinking a beer. The rest had cans of Fanta and Coca-Cola. They praised me for playing so well at the poolside party, pleasantly surprising them all after I had played shit at the rehearsal. The shit part came from Maleshoane.

Because she was ogling you, said one of the women. As if he had never seen a woman of substance before.

Trust the women to embarrass me.

What were you looking for, boy-child? asked Maleshoane. They say you were staring at me instead of backing Mme Mpuse. I didn't notice because I am paid to dance, not to look at men of the koriana.

The koriana is the accordion. That's what Basotho call it.

Maybe he was attracted by your dance, said another one.

While they laughed at me, I went to the counter and ordered two beers. I gave one to Maleshoane.

What about us? asked one of the women.

I chuckled and said I did not have money to waste on soft drinks. They merely laughed and called me a stingy leloabe. Their tone and sweet faces told me it was all in jest, not the way Moliehi, child of my mother, usually meant it.

After some time, the three women left while I plied Maleshoane with more beer. And regaled her with stories of my imagined greatness.

One day I will be an heir to Teboho Lesia, I said.

Never heard of him, said Maleshoane.

That's Famole, I said with a flourish.

She laughed for a long time, shaking her head pityingly. I didn't think I had said anything funny and was getting annoyed.

Why not just Famole? she asked. You use his real name and surname just to show off that you knew him personally and you were buddies?

She suggested that I knew Famole personally. Why would I disabuse her of that notion? Why would I tell her that I only admired the great kheleke from a distance, if it enhances my stature to her?

Yes, the one they called Famole, I said with so much pride in my voice. I am going to take Famole's greatness and wear it for myself like a soft warm blanket. I am going to walk, even dance, in Famole's gumboots.

He is a kheleke like any other kheleke, said Maleshoane with irritating irreverence.

He was a singer of peace for one thing, I said. He did not rap in lyrics that threatened others. He did not jump up and down with his stick raised doing the tlala dance. Or if he did tlala at all, it was in playfulness, showing graceful agility rather than machismo. He delighted in pure entertainment. Yet he was one of the great MaRussia in his own right. You can be of MaRussia and yet be full of peaceful songs. And peaceful dances. Until someone provokes you. And then you become a masumu snake that has been goaded out of its hole. That was the nature of Famole.

Like Mme Mpuse, said Maleshoane. She sings only of peace and other good things. Of rich grazing lands and magnanimous chiefs.

Only now when she is old and dignified, I said, showing off again. I know her very well. She is a homegirl from my village of Likhoele. She was herself a leader of MaRussia in her day. She was a woman of the gun.

By the time the night had aged we were full of laughter and she was Shoane instead of Maleshoane. But she refused to come with me to bless the night in my room. Instead she went to the room she shared with the three dancers.

After breakfast we sat in the hotel lounge watching television while waiting for transportation to drop us at the taxi rank before taking Mme Mpuse to her home in Qeme.

*

Boy-child returned home to find turmoil. I was returning with some money and a promise of a visit from Maleshoane. An empty promise perhaps. But a promise, nonetheless. A promise of bursts of showers from puffy clouds. She lived in Leribe and danced for various famo performers as a freelancer. I told her about our out-fit with Mohalalitoe and she promised that if we invited her, she would come without hesitation. I intended to ensure that she kept her promise.

I was also returning with a box of Swiss roll, the kind of cake that I heard Toloki loved to eat with scallions. We had some scallions in the garden, thanks to Moliehi, child of my mother. My hope was that Toloki would be appeased.

He was not.

You cannot buy me with a piece of cake, he said.

It's a whole loaf, I said.

Even a hundred loaves, he said. Not after you deserted me when I needed you most. But why am I surprised? It is fashionable for every-one to desert me these days.

I knew that the everyone he was talking about was Noria. I thought they would have reconciled by now, whatever the problem was.

Toloki told me Noria had become a stranger to him. Days passed without even a glimpse of her. She and Moliehi, my evil sister, he added venomously, locked themselves in that house and he did not know what witchcraft they were doing there.

You mean they don't even go to matlapeng? I asked, referring to answering the call of nature in the dongas but actually meaning the outside corrugated-iron toilet. What are they doing in there?

On occasion I have knocked, demanding to see Noria, said Toloki. They either ignore me or your evil sister shouts back to say they're still resting. Resting for what during the day? That's why I think they fly on a broom at night.

Don't they cook? Don't they eat?

I didn't wait for a response but went to knock at Moliehi's door. I heard the women giggle. I tried the door. It was bolted from the inside,

80

which was quite strange. She never locked the door, whether it was day or night. Even when she went to the fields, either to attend matsema work-parties or to cultivate our own fields, the door was never locked.

I turned to Toloki who had followed me to the door and shrugged my shoulders in helplessness.

He followed me as I walked to my hut.

You heard what happened? he asked.

You must have done something for her to be boycotting you like this, I said. Think. What could it be? Sometimes women hold you by the heart without expressing their grievance.

I am talking about the funeral, he said.

I was ashamed that I hadn't even asked him how things went at the funeral.

People died at that funeral, he blurted out in anger.

I hadn't heard of it. I came in a 4+1 – an unmetered sedan taxi-cab – instead of a regular minibus taxi. Though it was licensed to carry the driver and four passengers, I was the only passenger from Maseru to Likhoele. Thus, there were no fellow passengers from whom to hear the latest gossip as would have been the case in a minibus.

Toloki told me it was a big funeral, attended even by government ministers and military officers. Obviously, the musician was a very important person in political circles, which surprised Toloki. I for one was not surprised. Some politicians were highly involved in the wars of the musicians. A well-known politician even launched his party with the same colours as the Cult of the Train, and at their rallies they had accordion music blaring from powerful sound systems, with rows of men and women in matching uniforms per-forming beautifully choreographed dances that drew from those one could see on stages and on television screens performed by dancers of the hymn singers. So it was common cause that some leading musicians identified with particular parties, whether governing or in opposition, and had their music performed on their political campaigns. Sometimes the musicians appeared in person at these rallies and their followers went crazy with excitement. They would surely vote for a party endorsed by their favourite kheleke.

Toloki was sitting on the mound trying very hard to make his wails blend with the hymn – here we are talking of a church hymn, not the hymns of the wanderers – that the people around the grave were singing. A concertina or accordion would have been a fitting tribute at this moment because the deceased had himself been an accordion player in addition to being a singer of hymns.

The coffin was about to be lowered into the grave when the air was pierced by the sharp voice of a man singing a hymn of the wanderers about death that stalked even the dead. Men in purple blankets appeared from different directions. They were dancing a slow but graceful mohobelo dance movement. Everyone thought they were part of the funeral ritual. After all, the bereaved family had even engaged the services of a professional mourner. It must have been some of the new-fangled practices people who had money introduced to show off and make their funerals look different from those of their lowly neighbours.

The men's dance stopped right in front of the gaping grave. They took out machine guns from under their blankets and fired a few rounds in the air. Was it some kind of a salute for a fallen comrade? Some women screamed and a few men threw themselves to the ground. They must have seen that on television. The military officers and their bodyguards were caught off guard and for a while they froze.

The men in purple blankets pointed their guns at the church minister conducting the service and members of the congregation who were close to the grave.

A military officer yelled, Don't do anything stupid!

Let's hear what they want! said Toloki.

We have come to kill this man, said the balaclava-clad leader of the invading gang, now standing at the edge of the grave. He was pointing at the coffin.

I thought it was the most ridiculous thing, said Toloki, and I couldn't hold myself. I shouted at him, he is dead, you fool. How do you kill a dead man?

The man pointed his machine gun at Toloki and asked, Who are you, calling me a fool?

I am Toloki the Professional Mourner. You have disturbed a very sacred ritual of the dead.

I said that I was amazed at his bravado.

You may call it that, said Toloki. But what do you do when even soldiers are quivering?

One gangster pushed Toloki into the grave while the others demanded the coffin be opened. They wanted to shoot the dead man dead once more. They had been gunning for him for a long time after he led his gang against their illegal miners in Welkom. Unfortunately, a rival gang got him first, before they could deal with him, depriving them of the joy of killing the bastard. They demanded that his corpse be taken out of the coffin. No one dared touch the coffin. No one dared help Toloki as he attempted to claw his way out of the grave. Some pious woman started a hymn. A church hymn. That seemed to enrage the gangsters. Three of them fired a volley of shots at the coffin, leaving it, and certainly the man inside, in tatters.

Only then did the frozen bodyguards of military officers and cabinet ministers come to life and fire at the retreating gang members. The gang fired back. Innocent civilians were caught in the crossfire. Two villagers dead, five admitted to the government hospital in Mafeteng, one soldier dead, three policemen in ICU. Only two of the musicians in the purple blankets were arrested, both chorus singers and dancers for an unnamed kheleke.

People had their suspicions, but no one could identify the colour of the blankets, nor associate it with any known gang of musicians.

How did you escape the bullets? I asked.

I was still in the grave when it started, trying to climb up. I stayed right there, he said.

Your Balimo were great, I said, referring to his ancestors. They saved you from the grave with a grave.

I thought I had said something smart, but Toloki didn't seem to notice. He was shaking his head in bewilderment.

You famo musicians are a strange lot, he said. What recklessness is this, risking death or possible arrest just to kill someone who's already dead?

Just show-off, I said. It's more for the living. To spread terror to rival musicians. To show them that even in the midst of government ministers and military commanders they can get you. They are sending the message, never cross us. There's no escaping us. Even if you're dead we'll still come for you. We'll harass your bereaved family at your very funeral. Don't mess with us.

Since it was clear that Moliehi and Noria had no intention of coming out soon I rushed to a café and bought a loaf of white bread and two bottles of Fanta Orange. I sat with Toloki on a bench outside the mokhoro and we ate. From there I could see some cans of beef and of pilchards on the thothobolo ash-heap where we dumped rubbish.

You have been surviving on that? I asked.

They forgot my existence, Toloki said. Okay, once Moliehi brought me pap and wild spinach, but I refused to touch it, fearing it might be poisoned.

My sister would never do such a thing, I said. I couldn't hide my annoyance. Maybe that's why they stopped feeding you. I would too if you accused me of wishing to poison you.

A Land Rover stopped next to the corral. Two uniformed members of the Lesotho Mounted Police Service walked towards us. Toloki thought they were looking for him, perhaps to take a statement as a witness of the events at the funeral.

It is this one, said one of the policemen, patting me on the shoulder quite violently.

The second one handcuffed me.

What is the problem? What have I done?

What is he being arrested for? asked Toloki.

Without a further word the policemen led me to the Land Rover. I saw Toloki rushing to Moliehi's door, banging hard with both fists and shouting that the police were arresting me. They pushed me into the back of the van.

I could see through the meshed barred windows that the Land Rover was driving to Mafeteng. Soon the police would discover their mistake, I told myself. This must be a matter of mistaken identity. If it's about the funeral, I was not even there. I couldn't remember anything remotely criminal that I had done.

The police van stopped at a dilapidated house at Ha Ramokhele Township, next to a shebeen where men and women were sitting outside enjoying home-brewed beer and eating the boiled head of a sheep. The policemen unlocked my cuffs and ordered me to go into the house. I hesitated at the door. The policemen didn't follow me but got into their Land Rover.

Come on, go in. They are waiting for you, said one of them before driving away.

I knocked and someone said I should enter.

And there were Mohalalitoe, Mochini-oa-Ipommpa and three young men – boys, in fact – in brand-new purple seana-marena blankets with ornate edges. The boys were glistening in red ochre, which told me they were fresh graduates of the school of the mountain – the mophato.

Mohalalitoe was puffing on a thick zol of matekoane, the ancestral tobacco of the Khoikhoi and San people.

You sent the police to arrest me? I asked, without even greeting them first.

Not to arrest you. To invite you to join us over here, said Mohalalitoe. We don't have arresting powers. We are only musicians.

He passed the zol to Mochini who moistened its body with saliva before dragging smoke deep into his lungs.

They handcuffed me, man, I said.

Mochini found the whole thing funny and was giggling. Maybe it was the effect of the zol. I didn't know if the boys were amused too. They hid their mouths in their blankets.

I was fuming.

This is shit! My people are worried as we speak because they think I have been arrested. You can be sure by now the whole village thinks I am a criminal. What's the meaning of this? Just showing off that you have the police in your pocket?

The two men asked me to calm down. Mochini gave me the zol. I took only one weak drag and gave it back to him. I wanted to be sober when I dealt with these clowns.

Mohalalitoe said they summoned me to brief me on their progress since they went into hiding.

Firstly, Mohalalitoe was on the roll. That was the main thing they wanted to share with me. Mohalalitoe was on the roll.

It occurred to me that when they talked of Mohalalitoe they were not talking of the man but of the band itself. Lekhotla la Mohalalitoe. The Cult of the Arum-Lily. Patterned after the Cult of the Train. Mohalalitoe the man was modelling himself on Khosi Mosotho Chakela.

This had not been my understanding of our union.

But we said we were all equal partners, all three of us, I said. How come the group is named after you?

Mohalalitoe passed the zol. I shook my head. He gave me an it's-your-loss expression and puffed away happily.

We are still equal partners, he said. But there must be a face that leads from the front. I am that face. I am the one who is known to the rest of the koriana music world as the man who played with Khosi Mosotho Chakela, the man who was one of those at the fore-front of the Train.

We would name our outfit after you too, Moliehi's brother, if you had a beautiful name like Mohalalitoe, said Mochini. Mohalalitoe is a beautiful flower. Delicate. Sweet smell. Like the music we'll produce.

I was not going to argue with that. As long as Mohalalitoe understood he was not my boss. He could be Mochini's boss for all I cared. All I wanted was to be a kheleke of note, playing beautiful music, appearing on television. I wanted Radio Lesotho, Mo-Afrika FM, and Lesedi FM to play my hymns day in and day out. I, boy-child, was going to be a kheleke of the world whatever it took. If Mohalalitoe was the vehicle for that, so be it. After all, these were experienced men who had worked with the Train over the years and knew the ways of record companies, agents, music producers and concert promoters.

Mohalalitoe was now on the roll.

At first, when they had to be hidden by the deputy district commissioner, they thought it would be the end of them. They thought the long arm of the Cult of the Train would reach them wherever they were hiding. They even considered joining Letlama for better protection.

But I am tired of working under others, boy-child, said Mohalalitoe. I am determined to build my own outfit.

He kept on talking of it as his own outfit. Perhaps it was just a figure of speech.

Mohalalitoe was on the roll. They had even formed an alliance with an important mophato in Thabana Morena, and all the initiates had pledged allegiance to Mohalalitoe. The three graduates seated there were wonderful makhele singers. Mochini-oa-Ipommpa heard them when they were singing manngae – the songs of initiation-school graduands – and knew immediately that they would be the core of the chorus.

We should start rehearsing immediately, said Mohalalitoe. You will play the accordion, as will I. But yours, boy-child, will be the principal one because we recognised your superior fingers. We saw them in Bloemfontein where they even scared Khosi himself. Mochini will be on the drums. That is what he was born to do. You heard already how beautiful these young men are in the singing of makhele choruses. We're going to get more young men as they graduate from our mophato. Granted, we'll not be as big in terms of numbers as the Cult of the Train or any of the Letlama factions, but we'll make our mark. Word is going around already that no one should mess with us.

Mohalalitoe was on the roll.

Dancers, I said. I didn't hear you mention women dancers.

I don't want women dancers in my outfit, said Mohalalitoe. Women cause trouble. Haven't you seen the Cult of the Train doing memorable songs and hymns without women shaking their buttocks and distracting everybody?

But it is *our* outfit and I want women, I said. I realised immediately that I sounded like a bratty child and regretted it.

I want you to listen to Khosi Mosotho Chakela's 'Ke Hana Ke Holile', said Mohalalitoe.

I know that song, I said with disdain. Who doesn't know that song?

Do you see any women there? asked Mohalalitoe. It is one of the best performances you'll ever see. And it is all men.

You still admire Khosi Mosotho Chakela, I can see, I said.

I am talking about the song. It is beautiful. It is about old age. Yet it is a song of war. You don't see any woman prancing about there. You see old men glorying in the wisdom of their age. Old warriors who have seen times of war leading young men in four-part harmony – the present breed of warriors.

It is a beautiful song, added Mochini. Listen carefully to the drums. Those are my drums.

I have heard songs of war from Letlama, for instance, with women dancers in them. Women can be warriors too. Mme Mpuse was a woman of the gun.

She doesn't sing of war any more, said Mochini dismissively.

I don't want to sing of war either. I want to sing only of beautiful things, I said.

No one is going to stop boy-child from singing of beautiful things, said Mohalalitoe cajolingly. He who will be devoured by vultures, Moliehi's brother himself, no one can tell him not to sing of beautiful things. War is one of the beautiful things too, for it enhances your dignity as a musician. It protects your legacy. It makes others not shit on you. Audiences love a musician who is not a coward.

I mumbled to myself, I want women dancers.

5

Colours

Senyamo banana. I present myself to you, girls of Lesotho. I present myself as a suitor. Hold my gaze and love me. This dog is besotted with you, girls. Where are the cattle going, passing the graves even as diggers are digging them? Where are my father's herds going? If you were to die, I would dig you out of the grave. And continue to shower you with love. I am singing you this proposal song. I am sorghum, I spill out on the ground. I am a tin drum, I clang sharp notes of love. I burble and fizzle like water flowing in a furrow. I am a plank, I break into many pieces. I am a corrugated-iron roof, I shimmer in the sun. I shimmer from a distance in the sun. I shimmer in the moonlight. I shimmer under the stars. I shimmer on the darkest of nights.

Senyamo banana ba Matelile. Love me back, you girls of Matelile. Girls of Thabana Morena. Girls of Likhoele. Girls of the home of koriana. Girls of the Accordion Triangle. Give me the eye; return my love!

Each time the song mentioned a village, the women from that village cheered, whistled and the carefree ones performed the most daring of focho dances, legs flying so high they displayed the spotlight – the chalk circle drawn around the unclad Lesotho. In this case Lesotho did not refer to the country, as it did in my song, but to the woman's sacred place between the thighs.

Only those women who called themselves matekatse or mahure – whores – were brave enough to display the spotlight to the joyful laughter of everyone. Those whose hymns were full of self-praise for being the best whores that ever lived. Those who had taken the matekatse label that was meant to slut-shame them, and were defiantly using it to describe themselves, thus removing its sting and validating their humanity. Those who would one day boast to their grandchildren, my children's children, you see me looking like this, I was once a person in my day. I was a great whore running around with MaRussia in the City of Gold. It is a life you must never attempt to follow. It is sweet when it is happening, but when it has ended, as it is bound to end one day, it is bitter. Nights are gone, but you've reaped only glorious memories and tears of sorrow from them.

The rest of the women, most of whom envied matekatse but lacked their gumption, moved their bottoms rhythmically with decorum and delicate sensuality. Later they learned from the rewards that a subtle tease captured prospective lovers more effectively than the blatant display of a Lesotho. Nuanced men desire only what they cannot see, what is merely suggested, what appeals to imagination. A map. A hint.

I was used to having the spotlight flashed in my direction. I knew that my accordion had the tendency to charge bodies of revellers with unruly currents of elation. Impious recklessness. Bless the self-styled matekatse for showing their appreciation by performing the most high-flying focho.

I was inured to provocation. My heart was yearning for one person and she was in Leribe. I had sent messages: please come and join me, Shoane. Come and dance for Mohalalitoe. I meant the band, not the man. I had come to terms with calling our outfit Mohalalitoe despite myself. Though the Leribe person ignored my pleas, the thought of her made me invincible in front of the spotlight.

The men relished the spectacle and joined in the song, backing it in four-part harmonies – singing it in the makhele chorus style. Everyone is a performer at a famo party. Everyone is part of the spectacle. No one is a passive spectator.

When I got to lifela, the hymn part of the piece, the poetry recitation part, the part where any reveller could challenge me with his or her own hymn, the accordion assumed a life of its own. As usual. And the merrymakers went berserk. This was my favourite part. The part where I showed everyone that it was high time I was given the title of kheleke – the eloquent one.

For this particular song it was not my own eloquence that should be credited for it was not my composition, though I seasoned it with some of my words here and there, and some of my own koriana style.

Aoooo-oe-le-leee, take notice of me, girls of Mafeteng. I am a suitor. Where are the cattle going, Ntate Famole? This dog from Matelile loves you, girls with dimples on the cheeks. Look back, you have dropped something. Behind you, behind you, on the ground you've dropped something. Where are the cattle going, passing the graves even as the diggers are digging? If you were to die, the way I love you, girls of Lesotho, if you were to die, I would exhume you. I would use a gentle tool to dig you out of the grave because a pickaxe and shovel would hurt you.

Moliehi's brother, you have damaged Famole, said a woman after my hymn.

You have torn Famole to pieces, boy-child, said a man. You are truly the man to be divvied by vultures for breakfast.

The rest of the revellers agreed. Some chanted that I was a dog. Ntja e mmpe. A bad dog. An ugly dog.

All this praise was going to my head and I was becoming dizzy. The woman who owned the famo gave me a plastic container of pineapple beer, proclaiming that after such a breathtaking performance surely my dry throat needed some lubrication. The potent beer went to my head even more.

I needed some respite from the stenches of alcohol, sweat and tobacco. I placed my accordion between steel drums of pineapple and hops beer, and I went outside. As I was rolling my zol of Horseshoe Tobacco mixed with a few seeds of matekoane an impertinent voice said, you are wearing the colours of the Train and yet you steal Famole's song!

That was rubbish, of course! It was Famole's song and I never pretended otherwise. Even when I got to the hymn part where Famole sang of his name, calling himself a dog from Matelile, I did not substitute my name for his, as some performers did when they rendered cover versions of other musicians. I was informing even those who did not know that this was Famole's song, not mine. I was playing a Famole song not because I did not have my own. I was paying tribute to him. I was respectful of the dead man. Yes, I decorated it with my own words here and there, but essentially it was still his song. Our elders say you build a corral around the word of the dead. I say you build it around his music too.

Did you not hear my question, uena monna? asked my tormentor.

I heard it, I said curtly. But I don't answer stupid questions.

He was not alone. There were three others with him. Standing in the shadows. Their silhouettes leaning against their sticks.

You have the gall, Man of the Train, said the first man. You come here on our turf displaying the arrogance of your Cult. You have a liver!

As he said this he was rolling his blanket around the hand that held the stick that was going to be used as a shield. With the right hand he began to swing his second stick in my direction.

I have a liver, I said, preparing to face him. A very big one too. And it is not yellow.

It is as yellow as your blanket, shouted one of his allies. The rest of the allies burst out laughing, one of them urging his warring mate to show me my mother – an expression that meant he should beat me to a pulp.

Damn the accordion! Because I had it strapped to my shoulders and was playing it, most times I didn't carry a stick when I travelled. Every self-respecting Mosotho man carried a stick both as accoutrement and weapon. I carried music.

A man who was waiting for me to share my zol with him offered me his stick and I handed him my zol. I did not care that I didn't have a second stick to use as a shield. The single stick would serve both as weapon and shield. It was the way of Basotho stick fighting anyway. This thing of using two sticks, one a shield and the other a weapon, was an import from the Bathepu people. We are a one-stick nation.

I whistled, performed the tlala dance and then went straight for my challenger. I danced in circles around him as he tried to hit me. I ducked every blow. His friends egged him on. That infuriated me even more. I am boy-child. I am Moliehi's brother. He came with one killer blow, I heard it whoosh past my ear as I ducked to the side.

His own momentum hurled him to the ground. His stick was flung a few metres from him. I was on him with my stick. A few whacks on the head.

The whole famo party was now outside watching and cheering me on. You don't intervene when two men are facing each other in a fair fight.

The man was squirming on the ground. His friends charged and were on me with their sticks.

You cowards, shouted a woman. It was man to man, face to face. Now when your comrade has been defeated you all hit this boy-child!

I could see the stock of a rifle coming straight at my head, and darkness fell.

*

I had to die first, Shoane, I had to die before you could heed my call. I had to be killed by MaRussia before you could catch a 4+1 to Mafeteng to see me?

Do not cry to me like a baby, boy-child, I am not your mother, said Maleshoane. Plus, you are not dead yet. You have not been ripped to pieces by the vultures yet.

I could have died out there, I said.

But then I stopped myself immediately. Some women preferred a macho man who walked around beating his chest and talking shit to everybody. They believed arrogance was a virtue. But there were other women who liked to see a touch of humanity in a man. Something that said this man is capable of a teardrop. I did not know Maleshoane well enough to place her in either of the two categories. It was therefore best to stop playing the victim and moaning about nearly dying, lest she lose respect for me. I could do all the moaning to Moliehi, child of my mother.

I am glad you came, I said. Perhaps I should get beaten more often. That's the only way I'll get to see you.

I could see the patients on both sides of my bed leering at her. She looked quite regal, without the blonde wig, but with a red seshoeshoe doek matching her dress. Her face was embellished with lituba-tuba and menyetse, but it was obvious they were not the traditional marks that were permanently tattooed. Hers were drawn, perhaps with an eyebrow pencil. Even when she entered as soon as the visitors' time was announced, she excited me with her heavy steps on the wooden floor, as if she wanted to kill it. A gait that gave her so much gravitas my fellow patients and the nurses attending to them couldn't help but turn their heads in her direction.

Shoane didn't seem to be conscious of the effect she had. Or didn't care.

Where are you going to sleep? I asked her.

I will look for friends, she said. I have people I know. I have danced in every district of Lesotho.

You must sleep at my father's house, I said. Moliehi, child of my mother, will look after you.

She does not know me, said Shoane. She must not think I am one of the matekatse you picked up at a famo party. I will go to people who know me.

I was just making idle conversation, of course. There was no way I could ask Moliehi to give Maleshoane accommodation for the night. She might as well go to the people she claimed she knew. In any event, I was going to be discharged the next day. That's what the doctor promised. Well, a tentative promise, conditioned on the hope that there would be no deterioration in my condition. It was just a concussion, he said, and with the help of painkillers it would resolve itself on its own. However, since I came from nearby Likhoele

I could come to see the doctor again the following week as an out-patient. Just to make sure.

Mohalalitoe and Mochini-oa-Ipommpa entered the ward arguing with the nursing sister. Or so I thought. But when they got closer to my bed it turned out they were begging her to allow them in even though the visiting hour was almost over. They had urgent business connected with my injuries that they had to discuss with me. She parted with them at my bed, requesting them to hurry, and including Maleshoane in her gaze.

I asked Maleshoane not to leave yet because I wanted to introduce her to the two men.

Who did this to you? asked Mohalalitoe.

I do not know those men. I couldn't identify any of them.

What colours were they wearing? asked Mochini.

It was dark, I didn't see the colours. I am only sure about the blanket of the one I was giving his mother. It was a lefitori.

That doesn't help us much, said Mohalalitoe. What colour was it?

You can't distinguish colours properly when it is dark, I said, getting a bit exercised.

Where did it happen, man? asked Mohalalitoe, also losing his patience. Surely somebody must have seen those men.

Both men broke into a string of invective when I told them it was at a famo in Thabana Morena where I was playing. I was taken aback.

Why are you angry with me? I asked. I am the victim here.

You are a naïve village boy. Your talent means nothing if you continue to be stupid like this. You belong to Mohalalitoe now. You cannot play at a famo party like a common koriana player. You cannot play at focho parties. You cannot play at weddings and village feasts. Otherwise you would be spoiling the name of the Cult of the Arum-Lily.

Spoiling it for whom? I asked, genuinely puzzled. No one knows anything about us.

Speak for yourself, said Mochini.

I am speaking for myself. I am the one who was playing at a famo, and no one tells me what to do. I bring merriment wherever I want. Or do you people think I am going to ask you to fight my battles for me against those assailants? I, boy-child, can stand up for myself.

I could see the veins in Mohalalitoe's neck threatening to burst. I still didn't understand what the big deal was. He was battling to calm himself. And he succeeded. He shushed Mochini who was railing about my lack of intelligence. And then he turned to me and slowly and deliberately explained, as if he was talking to an imbecile, that Mohalalitoe was starting from the highest level. In the big leagues. No one must see it or talk of it as an up-and-coming band. Right from the very beginning it must be treated with the same respect as the Cult of the Train, the Red Letlama, the Black Letlama and other outfits of that stature. These highly respected outfits must see it more as a rival than a group of upstarts. Rivals in music, in war and in mining.

By playing at a famo party I was demeaning the brand.

What do you think it would do for Khosi Mosotho Chakela to be seen playing at a famo party in Matelile Ha Makhakhe? asked Mohalalitoe.

Why not? I asked. Mme Mpuse has played at a feast in Likhoele.

That was her own feast, said Mohalalitoe. And she was just being gracious.

I can be gracious too, I said.

You are not famous enough to be gracious, said Mohalalitoe.

Yes, I am not a star like Khosi Mosotho Chakela, I said. I am a man of the people. I am a wanderer, a rambler who is fuelled by the korostina and the koriana to cross valleys and entertain people in villages beyond the mountains.

You are a star when you are with Mohalalitoe, whether you know it or not. From now on I do not want to hear that you played at a famo or any kind of timiti. Unless you want to forgo the kheleke title that Mohalalitoe was going to bestow on you. Unless you do not want to cut albums and be a big name on radio and television. Unless you do not want to feature in festivals of thousands in the big stadiums of South Africa.

I did want all those things. I gave in by keeping quiet, pretending I was sulking. But if this was the only road to stardom open to me at that point, I would have to toe the line.

Is this gifted woman your sister Moliehi? asked Mochini.

I had noticed that even as I was being berated, he was leering at Shoane. And she was looking him straight in the eye as if daring him. A pinch of jealousy. Relief when he failed to keep up the dare.

Ask him why he doesn't ask me himself, said Shoane, addressing the words to me.

She is Maleshoane from Leribe, I said.

I was not saying you should answer for me, said Shoane.

I answer because he asked me, I said. She's going to be one of our dancers, I added, looking at Mohalalitoe, whose veins suddenly returned to his neck.

Dancers? he screamed. I thought we sorted that out. We are not going to have women dancers. Only men. Men who have been to the school of the mountain.

What do you have against women? asked Shoane.

I love them. I married a few, said Mohalalitoe. But I prefer male dancers.

I prefer women dancers, I said. Or both. Men and women. Like those I have seen in the music of Lekase, the revered leader of the main Letlama group. Have you seen Lekase's 'Monna Moholo'? Have you seen those women dance, sticks raised and breasts heaving? Lekase is deadly in songs and hymns. He is deadly in fighting as well. That is why he is called Lekase – Coffin. Yet he does not think women dancers make him a sissy. I hear your reason when you say I must stop playing famo. But your reason against women dancers is stupid. We are going to have women dancers. Or our journey ends here. Before it becomes long.

You are bringing matters of love into our business, I can see that, said Mohalalitoe weakly. That is dangerous. That is dangerous.

Mochini parroted, Dangerous. Very dangerous.

Mohalalitoe was giving in. I was not about to give him a second victory in one day. I could see he was giving in. Shoane looked at me with new-found respect. She obviously hadn't thought I could stand my ground with these men who had seen much bigger things than I had.

Mohalalitoe wanted to go back to my playing at the famo.

I thought we were done with that, I said.

Not until you tell me why you were wearing Khosi Mosotho Chakela's blanket, said Mohalalitoe.

Is he perhaps a traitor? asked Mochini. Does he still yearn to join the Cult of the Train, though we have an agreement?

Are you working with the Train people? asked Maleshoane.

I was wearing my blanket, not Chakela's. Long before Khosi Mosotho Chakela was born the black and yellow colours, sometimes called black and gold to give yellow more lustre, represented the district of Mafeteng. They had always been the colours of the district soccer team, Bantu FC, the Black Matebele. The Train people had appropriated them, and I was resentful that I was being questioned for wearing them.

I had been puzzling the motive of my attackers since I regained consciousness yesterday. I couldn't figure out who they were. I remembered one mentioning the Train. If they were accusing me of being a member of the Cult of the Train because of the colours of my blanket, then they belonged to a rival gang. It could be any one of the gangs. I could say one of the Letlama groups because they were known for their viciousness. But the man who was on the ground while I was giving him his mother was not wearing a letlama. It was clearly a lefitori, also known as the Victoria blanket after the dead Queen of the British Isles. Though I could not distinguish the colours clearly because of the dark, I remembered seeing the ornate crown designs that embellished the blanket as he was squirming on the ground.

Unless they were of the Train. The man seemed to hate the fact that I was wearing what he referred to as the Train blanket while I played Famole, a well-known rival of Khosi Mosotho Chakela. The squirming man's blanket was of the brand that could be worn by Chakela's men, though the colours were much darker – perhaps blue, brown, green, but certainly not yellow. I would have distinguished yellow even in that dimness.

I was a victim of colours. It had happened to many other people. You were at the wrong place at the wrong time wearing the wrong colours. Innocent colours. Not only colours of the blankets, but even T-shirts. And then some thugs attacked you because they thought you belonged to a rival gang of musicians. Or you were a supporter of a rival music group. The war of the musicians had spilled over to innocent civilians, and people were dying because of colours.

It infuriated me that my blanket was being stigmatised. As if Khosi Mosotho Chakela and his Cult of the Train had bought it for me. Or as if they invented it. My blanket was my own. It used to be my father's blanket. My only inheritance from him. Okay, I inherited cattle as well. But they got finished. A combination of my reckless-ness and the rustlers who knew there was no man in the homestead as I was rambling the land with my concertina. Rambling while Moliehi, child of my mother, tilled the soil and looked after the cattle.

The blanket was my only remaining inheritance.

I valued that blanket and would not allow the Cult of the Train to claim authority over it. Nor would I let those who wanted to read their own meaning into it win the day. It was my father's seana-marena. My father and I brought it in Leribe when I was a teenager. A few months before the table fell on him.

He was home on leave from the land of the White man, other-wise known as Makhooeng. Mohala oa cheche, the bush telegraph, reached Likhoele, as it did every corner of Lesotho, that Mr Robertson, a Hlotse Leribe businessman famous for the Basotho blankets that he ordered from England, was expecting new stock of seana-marena blankets the following week. My father had always wanted one, so he decided to go to Leribe that Sunday. Because the only place outside Likhoele I had ever been to was the camp of Mafeteng I asked to go with him. My mother also thought it would do me a load of good to see other places outside our district.

I could still remember the journey very well. We walked to the camp of Mafeteng – it was before the days of 4+1 and minibus taxis – where we caught a bus called Ikaneng Bus Service at the market-place. I remember it moving very slowly and stopping at every little village along the road to Maseru. At the Maseru bus stop, also near a marketplace, I had never seen so many people in my life. Vendors selling all kinds of goods and foods swarmed around the bus. My father bought me leqebekoane steamed bread and a piece of fish battered in a thick layer of spiced dough.

We took another bus from Maseru to Teyateyaneng, and yet another one to the border town of Maputsoe. Each bus stop was bustling with people – passengers with heavy baggage, some with children in tow, and peddlers of every conceivable product. At every bus stop the dominant food was fish and steamed bread, oranges and apples. At every bus stop there was a man or men who played either the korostina or the koriana – concertina or accordion. These musicians always seemed to be carefree and were surrounded by happy admirers.

Though we did not change buses in Maputsoe I could see people buying songs from the accordion player and I thought it was a wonderful kind of job. They stuck money on his forehead, which he allowed to fall on the ground. Most requested a specific song. He played their requests and they danced happily.

He was a purveyor of happiness and that left a lasting impression in my mind. I saw myself in him. Not because he was making money. That didn't enter my mind even though I could see the coins accumulating in front of him. It was just the idea of being the cause of so much joy, of young women giggling and dancing, of crowds surrounding him, applauding, cheering, joining in a singalong. Once one had bought a song, it was enjoyed by everyone. Even those who did not have money. The whole idea of sharing a song with the less fortunate fascinated me.

It took us the whole day to get to Hlotse, the capital town of the Leribe district. It was Sunday evening, but the line from the veranda of Robertson's general dealer's store was already long. People coming from all corners of Lesotho already queuing for the seana-marena blanket. We spent the night outside in the queue on the roadside, amidst jokes and laughter.

Robertson opened at eight in the morning and stood on the veranda in his khaki shirt and shorts. He announced that it would take a while to open for everyone as they first had to sort the blankets: separate those that were pre-ordered and prepaid by the important people according to their colours, and then those that were going to be gifted to the royal family and to each one of the principal chiefs of Lesotho. Every principal chief deserved to have a seana-marena, and some of them had the blankets by the dozen. Accumulated over the years from the days of the senior Robertson who was reputed to have designed a number of blankets that had become iconic, including seana-marena.

Only after that would we, the vulgus, the mahoo-hoo in other words, be allowed to purchase our colours of choice.

When we returned home the next day, my father had his yellow-and-black seana-marena – the colours of Bantu FC and of the district of Mafeteng – in a soft plastic wrapper.

On our way to Leribe my father did not speak much except to ask if I wanted something to eat or if I was thirsty for a bottle of ginger beer that the women were selling. I was not expecting much talking from him anyway; he was a brooding man even at home. Except when he was with his friends at some feast or funeral. We heard rumours that he was the life of the party. But immediately he got home he clammed up.

On our way back, however, my father was talking non-stop, holding his beloved seana-marena blanket close to his bosom. He pointed at the things he saw outside the window and gave his opinion on them. He commented on the beautiful houses by the road-side. On the ugly ones too. He joked that he was going to sell me to some man who was pushing a sheep on a wheelbarrow – obviously to a place of slaughter – and laughed out loud at his joke. I chuckled a bit though it was not funny.

After we had changed to Ikaneng Bus Service in Maseru our conversation took a serious turn. He wanted to know what I wanted to be when I grew up. I always found such a question stupid. What else would I want to be but what every man in the village, including him, was? A grown-up. We grew up herding cattle. Those of us who were fortunate went to school, perhaps up to the end of lower primary school where we learned to write at the very least our names. And then some of us went to the initiation school where we were circumcised into men. But those of us whose parents were staunch Christians, especially Catholics, shunned the mophato lest they be excommunicated by the Fathers. The next stop for us, whether circumcised or not, would be The Employment Bureau of Africa, known to us as Teba, where we joined the labour force to the mines of South Africa. Mostly only the girls would finish higher primary and even go to high school. For most of the boys, the manly thing was to go to the mines.

I had to think of a quick answer.

I want to play the koriana, I said.

What kind of a job is that? he asked.

I saw that man at Maputsoe, I said. He was making a lot of money. And all he did was make people happy.

My father said only the maloabe played the koriana. I needed to strive to be an important person. A person of means. A respected person. A person who would not stand in the queue to buy a blanket, after sleeping on the pavement the whole night. A person who would have blankets put aside for him. And even delivered to his own house as Robertson surely must do for the principal chiefs.

I cannot choose for you what you should be after I have failed to be anything but a mineworker, he said finally. But whatever it is, be best at it. So that you can look after my homestead when I am gone. And after your mother if I go before her. And after your sister, Moliehi.

When you go where, father? I asked.

People go, boy-boy. They don't live forever.

When we got home he stored his blanket in a kist and clammed up again. You would say I was lying if I told you he was conversation-personified on our way back from Leribe.

He wore his blanket only on very special occasions. For instance, when King Moshoeshoe II visited Mafeteng, my father and other men of the villages in the Accordion Triangle rode their horses to town. The men were all resplendent in their yellow-and-black blankets. Their thoroughbred Basotho ponies cantered in unison, led by a poet on a white horse reciting the praises of His Majesty. The horsemen then formed a guard of honour when the King's motorcade entered the town. Women ululated and children ran alongside the well-fed horses.

The proud horsemen from my village did not ride only on those occasions the King came to Mafeteng – and he visited a few times in my youth because Mafeteng was his wife's home – but also when Morena Leshoboro Seeiso, the principal chief of Mafeteng, also known as the Chief of Likhoele since his headquarters were in my village, rode to an important event. My father would then take out his seana-marena from his kist and join his fellow horsemen. The Basotho ponies trotted, cantered and galloped in unison as the riders displayed their horsemanship and their colourful blankets.

My mother was the first to go. My father lost his enthusiasm for horsemanship. The blanket stayed in the kist. And then the table fell on him. If his body had been brought home I would have made sure he was buried wearing that blanket. But he was never brought home. His body was never recovered under the rockfall.

It was Moliehi who made me wear the blanket many months after my father's passing.

Is it going to sit there in the kist until it rots? she asked.

Blankets don't rot, I said.

Who taught you that? Why do you think we put moth balls in the kist?

The first time I wore that seana-marena I was quite self-conscious. I was like a trespasser. But after I went to a timiti wearing it and I received much praise for its beauty both from men and women, I wore it a few more times. Especially when I wanted to take the children, ho nka bana, an expression we used for gaining popularity with the girls.

I had not been to a famo for quite some time. I wore it when I went for merriment in Thabana Morena. I never imagined that one day my father's prized blanket would be the death of me.

You are not dead yet, Maleshoane said once more.

*

After I had been discharged from the hospital Mohalalitoe and Mochini dropped us outside the gate. I was with Maleshoane. I smuggled her into my hut. At that time of the evening, I knew Moliehi would already be in her bedroom in the main house. We always teased her that she slept with the roosting chickens. Toloki, perhaps with Noria if they had reconciled, would be sitting outside the mokhoro, brooding about death and how to celebrate it by mourning it. Or perhaps Noria would already be on the bedding between bags of corn and beans. Listening to herself.

108

Most likely Toloki saw me getting out of the car with the woman. Knowing him, he would mind his business and not start blabbing about it to Moliehi. Or even to his partner who would be sure to tell my sister that ke koaletse, which meant I had locked myself in the house with a woman. But when I cast my eyes in the direction of the mokhoro, no one was sitting on the bench.

Although Shoane kept on reminding me that I had not yet earned her body she became very generous that night. Perhaps because I told her that she had not earned mine either. It had to be a two-way street: I earned, she earned. It was the way of the world.

A dancer is a dancer even on the moseme mat in the deep of the night.

In the morning I urged Shoane to stay inside the house until the afternoon when Mohalalitoe would pick us up for rehearsals. I would prepare sorghum sour porridge for her which she would eat with bread. It shouldn't be difficult to stay indoors until I could smuggle her out a few hours later. She didn't understand why I was hiding her.

Are you ashamed of me? she asked.

I don't want Moliehi to see you.

Is she your mother? she asked. Are you not a grown man? And then she giggled and added, Have you turned into a boy in the morning after you showed me manly flames in the night?

Of course she's not my mother, I said adamantly. We just respect each other. Always have. I never bring women here and she never brings men.

Toloki was sulky. I thought it was because he had not mourned since the day of the mass shooting. I thought his body was crying for a good dose of grief. But no, it was for something different. Okay, the lack of mourning had its part. But the major reason was Noria.

It turned out the situation between them had not changed from what it had been before I left for that famo party at Thabana Morena. And Toloki was distraught.

But there is nothing I can do about it, he said as he led me to the bench outside the mokhoro. I have decided to go overseas on my own and advance the cause of mourning the dead. To me, mourning is a calling. Apparently to her it was merely a labour of love. She followed me to various cemeteries because at the time she thought she loved me. Or it was for whatever she could get from me. But now it is clear that the love no longer exists. Perhaps it never existed in the first place. Perhaps it was just the sentimentality of homegirl meeting homeboy in a city far away from their village where they had shared a common story. She fascinated me, boy-child, for she wielded so much power over my father's creativity. My father could only create figurines to her song. For a while I thought that enchantment had been transferred to me. Mourning was lucrative while she managed me. And her love could not be doubted. Until we came here. Until she met your sister who led her astray.

He uttered these words, and I listened silently. I did not interrupt. I did not even clear my throat when he was putting all his woes at my sister's door. I could not imagine how Moliehi, child of my mother, was to blame if his woman no longer wanted to share blankets with him.

But you can't leave Noria here, I said. You brought her here. You must leave with her.

She has told me already that she no longer wants to go in search of mourning with me. She says she has discovered new ways of living, in a different realm from the ways of dying that I celebrate and mourn. She wants to stay here. Are you sure you have nothing to do with this?

I did not blame him for grasping at straws, even if those straws were me. A few moments ago it was Moliehi's fault, now it was mine. It's everybody's fault but Noria's.

Hey, you woman, who are you and why are you using my toilet? That was Moliehi's voice.

I'll tell you when I come back from using it. That was Maleshoane's voice.

I rushed to see what was happening. Moliehi was standing at the bottom of the rough stone steps that led to her stoep and Noria was standing at the door. Both were arms akimbo. Maleshoane was already in the corrugated-iron toilet.

What is your problem? asked Moliehi.

They say the best defence is attack.

You didn't even come to see me when I was in the hospital, I said. I could have died there, and you didn't care.

Do you know her? asked Moliehi.

She came to see me *at the hospital* when you didn't, I said. She's my visitor.

Maleshoane walked out of the toilet.

One of you get me a mug of water so that I can wash my hands, she said.

Just like that. As if she belonged here. As if she was one of us and had been living with us all our lives. As if she was our mother. Noria, without thinking twice about it, responded to her instruction by dashing into the house and returning with a mug of water. She walked down the steps to where Maleshoane was standing and slowly poured the water on her hands. She washed them and dried them by waving them in the air. Without so much as a thank-you.

Moliehi just stood there as if waiting for Maleshoane to say something. As did I. As did Noria. Toloki had joined us as well. But he was careful to distance himself by a few feet. Like an uninvited child from the neighbourhood. A child who had been told to go to his own home because we were about to dish up dinner.

Maleshoane laughed mockingly and said, He told me to hide myself in the house so that his little sister doesn't see me. What's wrong with you, little sister? Which one is she? The one who gave me water or the one who is staring at me as if I am a ghost from her past?

Noria giggled. Moliehi joined her. Chutzpah can be funny.

And you, said Maleshoane looking at me, have you seen your house lately? It is not a mansion with a toilet inside. Where did you think I was going to relieve myself while in hiding? You don't even have a chamber pot or a slop bucket.

The women broke out laughing. Toloki looked at me pityingly. I guffawed in his direction, obviously to communicate the fact that hey, you don't have to pity me. You are the pitiful one.

He walked back to his bench in front of the mokhoro. I just stood there marvelling at the chemistry that was brewing among the three women.

Maleshoane requested that they assist her with unbraiding her hair since she wanted to comb it into an afro when she went to the rehearsal in the afternoon.

Noria brought a bench from the house and placed it on the elevated stoep. Both women busied their fingers with undoing Shoane's tight braids. I sat on the stoep, my feet dangling.

In no time the women were laughing like old friends. When Shoane accused them of not going to see their brother at the hospital when she was able to come all the way from Leribe, a hundred and seventy kilometres away, to visit a man who was nearly killed by thugs, Moliehi explained that they did not know about it until yesterday afternoon when people from Thabana Morena came to return his accordion. They reported that he was carried on a donkey cart to the hospital at the camp after being attacked by rival musicians.

Why do you think we woke up so early today? Moliehi asked, looking at me, but providing an answer herself. We were preparing to go to check him at the hospital only to find out this morning that he had been discharged and was hiding a woman in his room.

This called for another round of laughter led by Shoane.

I was just happy that my accordion was back. I had planned to ask Mohalalitoe to take me to Thabana Morena to the famo house where I had left it between the drums of beer.

Where is my accordion now? I asked. Suddenly my fingers were itching for it.

Toloki took it, said Noria. He feels you don't appreciate it enough if you can just leave it at a timiti. He wants to trade it in to pay for his ticket to go overseas.

He's holding my accordion hostage for that? Didn't he give it to me as a gift?

Maleshoane laughed and said, All you men are like that. When love is gone you demand everything back. As if the gifts were a mere loan. I was once married. When I left him because the sound of the accordion was ringing in my head, he demanded back everything he ever bought me. Even snaps of himself that he had given me when love was in full bloom.

So you see, said Moliehi. You left him for no good reason, that's why.

Blame the accordion, said Maleshoane, and the focho dance. It was a mistake to marry him in the first place. I learned my lesson. For instance, I love your brother, but I would never marry him. Why would I want to spoil everything by marrying him?

It was a revelation that she loved me. She never told me that. She didn't tell me that when she danced for Mme Mpuse in Maseru. She didn't tell me that when she visited me at the hospital yesterday. She didn't tell me that when we danced the night away last night. And she just throws it now like a nonchalant bomb, and even rejecting a marriage proposal that I never made!

I left them there to negotiate the release of my accordion with Toloki. He was sitting on his lonely bench getting increasingly irritated by the laughter of the three women. I could hear it too and it was beginning to annoy me.

I am not giving you the accordion back, said Toloki. I need every cent I can get for it towards my ticket. Your family has damaged me.

Okay, lend it to me then while you are still here, I pleaded. I'll ask my band to pay for it. I promise you will have your money back.

You have a band? That's why you no longer want to mourn with me?

The women burst into another round of laughter. I was curious what it could be about. I was getting a bit jealous. Moliehi had robbed Toloki of his Noria. She must not rob me of my Maleshoane.

After extracting a promise from Toloki that he would rent the accordion to me for a small fee before someone paid for it outright, I walked back to the women. I was not sure whether to sit or pretend I was not interested in anything going on there and was going to my hut. But before I could decide, Moliehi called after me, laughing. Shoane tells us that the way you are so tiny compared to her big body, last night it was like a mouse sitting on a loaf of bread.

Once more the women broke into laughter. I was scandalised. I had never joked about anything sexual with Moliehi. There were boundaries between us, an older brother and a younger sister. Though she tended to mother me. Though she was the breadwinner most of the time. Still there had to be boundaries. And here came Maleshoane, obliterating them in one fell swoop.

114

I laughed back, with less enthusiasm, and said, Uena Shoane, you are a bad influence.

They were now combing her hair so that it stood up like Don King's.

I will look good at that rehearsal, said Shoane. Boy-child, did you know that your sister and her friend want to be dancers too? They want to sing the choruses of the hymns and dance like I do.

Not Moliehi, I said. Moliehi, child of my mother, was not created to dance for men.

You are not my father, said Moliehi. I will dance when I want to dance. And I do want to dance. How come Maleshoane can dance and we can't?

Maleshoane has been dancing all her life. That's her profession. You hated the koriana and famo music. You hated my korostina. You hated things of the night, as you called them. What happened?

You must give other children a break, said Maleshoane.

Not in my outfit. Not in my band. Not in the Cult of the Arum-Lily.

There's even a Cult? exclaimed Maleshoane. You're like the Train now?

Not this child of my mother, I said ignoring her question about our ambition to be like the Men of the Train. How would I answer to my grandmothers, those who are in the ground, when they ask how I allowed their granddaughter to be a vagabond? How would I answer to my father whose spirit is still trapped in a gold mine? My sister, this sister of mine, shall not be eaten by vultures while I am alive.

Moliehi seemed to be taken aback by the force of my emotions.

No vulture will touch her, said Noria. I will protect her.

With what of yours? I asked.

Yes, with what? That was Toloki. I had not noticed he had returned from his self-exile on the bench and had been listening to the argument.

115

You, Noria, should be going with your husband to mourn the dead instead of influencing my sister to do things she used to loathe before.

We can recapture our lives again, Noria, said Toloki. We can go back to our township if you are not keen on going overseas. We can go back to our township and home village and mourn death to our hearts' content.

I no longer want to associate with death, Toloki, said Noria, tears filling her eyes but refusing to run loose down her cheeks.

Perhaps if you give up mourning, get a piece of land and plant vegetables she would have you back, I said to Toloki.

I cannot do that, said Toloki. Even if I wanted to I could not do it. For me mourning is a sacred calling. I am a votary of the Sacred Order of Professional Mourners. Noria knew all that when we got together after I mourned her son Vutha. She encouraged me and managed my affairs.

Maleshoane was getting impatient. She did not care about the vagaries of mourning and the anguish of this strange man. She wanted Moliehi and Noria to fulfil their hearts' desire. She wanted them to be her companions on the stage, singing choruses and dancing for some great kheleke of the world. She kept on repeating that I should give other children a break.

I had to put my foot down. Otherwise Maleshoane would end up calling all the shots in my life. I put my foot down on this one.

Not in Mohalalitoe, I stressed each syllable. Not in any other band. This child, my mother's child, shall not be a famo dancer.

6

When I don't say anything it doesn't mean I don't feel anything

You pipsqueaks are descendants of MaRussia of old. They used to fight with sticks. With knobkerries. Ea-lla koto. We, old MaRussia, obtained our stature on the battlefield. The blood-soaked fields of Newclare. Of Phiri. Of Mapetla. Of Senaoane. Of New Canada. You, on the other hand, gain your stature through music.

But when you get to the Land of Gold, Gauteng, Maboneng, the City of Lights, you discover you have to defend your music through fighting. So, fighting will never leave MaRussia alone. As long as there are those who want to take away something from you. As long as there are those who are jealous of your hymns. As long as there are men and women out there who feel entitled to a slice of what you make from record deals, there will always be men who want to eliminate you. Meharo. Greed is the reason likheleke of accordion music try to eliminate one another.

The old man paused. He took a swig of sorghum beer from an old-style billycan. He grimaced at the sourness of his drink. He looked at me. But I was told that he could not see me. He was looking in the direction of my voice. Or of my scent. The little boy who acted as his eyes sat at his feet in front of him. Like a pet puppy.

I do not want to eliminate anyone, I said. There is room for us all. No one musician can finish all the followers in the world.

You may not want to eliminate anyone, but they will still want to eliminate you. And those followers you are talking about, they are often the problem. After eating your music until they are drunk with it, they want dust to rise. And not only from dancing feet. They want to smell one another's armpits in combat. The fickle bastards, sons and daughters of mahure! Offspring of Diablo!

Don't be hard on them, Tau ea Khale, I said, calling him by the endearment that all aged Basotho men love, Lion of Old. We get our livelihood from those very fickle bastards, those children of Liabolosi.

I was laughing all the while at his feigned indignation with everyone, ranging from the musicians to their fans. The face betrayed only warmth.

But it was not like that in our day, continued Tau ea Khale, ignoring my amusement. Warriors were warriors and musicians were musicians. We only saw musicians at night when we went to nurse our wounds and bruised egos at good-time places after the war had been won or lost. Today musicians are the commanders in the battlefield. Those not gifted in the art of war send out lieutenants to fight their battles. The astute ones have turned their fan base into marauding hooligans killing fellow Africans for wearing the wrong colours.

Tau ea Khale took a long gulp. The veins in his neck wiggled joyfully.

This thing is very new, he said. It only started around 1999 and escalated around 2007. I was in prison when I heard of it. New inmates sentenced to years because they killed others over music told us of the deaths that were happening outside. All of them Basotho. Mosotho killing another Mosotho for a song. Most of them from the same villages. From Matelile, Thabana Morena, Likhoele. Children of a man, boys who used to look after cattle together.

Today, you cannot be a gang leader unless you are a musician.

I knew if I came to Senaoane I would find this aged one who carried in his wrinkled body memories of a bygone era and in his battered face wisdom of the ages. He used to be my father's friend and was so full of shit in his youth he killed a man in a fight over a woman and spent ten years at Sun City Prison. He was paroled after going blind, and when he got out my father was already buried under rocks in some White man's mine. But, I was told, Tau ea Khale knew people who knew exactly the mine and the shaft that became my father's grave.

They tell me you are the new Famole, said Tau ea Khale, removing the foam from his mouth with the back of his hand.

I was chuffed. My reputation had reached the Basotho of Soweto even before I had cut a single record.

There can only be one Famole, Tau ea Khale, and I was there when we buried him in Matelile Ha Sekhaupane.

You did not bury him, said the old man. You only buried his bones, and his flesh which has since been eaten by the worms of the earth. The true Famole lives among us, walks among us. Otherwise how would you say we hear the voice of the dead singing for us the hymns of the wanderers? No, child of my friend, you did not bury Famole.

I could not contradict his word.

When you are a kheleke of Famole's stature, he said, death is impossible.

Death was impossible, not only because of his voice that continued to linger above the ground. Groups that professed his name emerged after we buried his avatar. One of them, the blue-blanketed men, evolved into the feared Letlama that was now in two factions, maybe three. Famous for their brutality among themselves and towards others, I hated these groups for muddying the name of my hero. I was told their members hated me too for being called the new Famole. As if I named myself that. As if I never tried to stop Mohalalitoe from billing me as such on its banners and posters. As if I was keen to carry that mantle on my shoulders when I knew it would be burdensome and would impinge on my free spirit. As if I didn't hate it when I heard people say, this boy-child who calls himself the new Famole is a disgrace; Famole would never do this, or Famole would never say that.

It was clear that Tau ea Khale was enjoying my presence. He insisted that I spend the week I was scheduled to be in Johannesburg at his house.

I am here for work, Tau ea Khale, so I thought since I am in Johannesburg anyway I might as well see my father's friend and get advice on how I can retrieve his bones from the White man's mineshaft so that his loved ones can give him a proper burial at Likhoele and he can then become a happy ancestor.

Who is stopping you from going to work? asked the old man, shaking his head as if I had uttered something stupid. Go to your work and come back to your home here. I am your father's friend and I am giving you a pillow to lay your head on. We could also use that time to locate some of the men who worked at the same mine with him and may remember which winze or raise collapsed on him.

I told the aged one that I was grateful for his generosity. But I hoped I would not be an inconvenience as I might return at very odd hours, as musicians are wont to do. I was in Johannesburg with Mohalalitoe to record some songs for *Ezodumo* television programme at the invitation of the great presenter and producer, Welcome Bhodloza Nzimande himself. After that, Mohalalitoe, the band, had an appointment with a record company to record a CD to be produced by Mohalalitoe, the man, who, as I learned only recently, was a top-notch producer of indigenous music. He had been responsible for some of the Cult of the Train's enduring hits. Those two main engagements might take many hours of the day and night, and I would hate to come back in the early hours of the morning and wake everybody up.

We are used to it, said the old man. The offspring of Diablo wake us up all the time. We live on the main street, which is busy day and night with drunkards and whores.

It was a red-brick four-roomed matchbox township house on Mabalane Street, the long street that linked the three townships of Mapetla, Phiri and Senaoane. They might be seen as one by a stranger as he wouldn't know where one township ended and the next one began. The house had a nostalgic feel to it, with a rusty corrugated-iron roof that still had the suggestion of red paint, and under big burglar-proofed windows, a cement stoep that used to be polished red when it was still fashionable to do so, but was now neglected and cracked.

The three townships were brimming with Basotho people, and most of the offspring of Diablo he was complaining about were descendants of old MaRussia who would nevertheless be ignorant of that history.

Another thing, Tau ea Khale, I said. There is a woman.

Where?

She is arriving tomorrow with the rest of the band. I do not know if you will consider it proper if I stay with her here. She is called Maleshoane from Hlotse Mankoaneng in Leribe.

Tau ea Khale's eyes, who had been sitting silently as if he was not there, shifted uncomfortably, and then he excused himself, saying that he was going to drink water. He was well brought up with good manners; he knew that when old people talk naughty things you leave the room.

Have you taken out cattle for her? the old man asked.

I was impressed that he was choosing his words well, respecting the Sesotho language. A careless man would have asked if I had *paid* any cattle for her. You don't pay cattle for a woman as if you are buying her. U ntša likhomo. You take out cattle for her.

I am not married, Tau ea Khale, I said.

Why not?

I do not think a man who is a wanderer like me should take a wife, I said. I don't want to marry for the walls of my father's house. I do not want loafers and dandy fuckboys to eat my father's cattle while I am singing hymns in distant towns.

The old man shook his head pityingly and said, They can eat her, but they won't finish her. When you return from your wanderings she will still be there, with her thing intact. It never gets finished.

Jo! This thing that Tau ea Khale was saying! An idea struck me right there. That could be a song. A hymn. A new hymn I would sing the next day at the *Ezodumo* taping. As soon as Mohalalitoe, Mochini-oa-Ipommpa and the dancers arrived we would rehearse it and, in the afternoon, we would tape it with the rest of our repertoire before a live studio audience at the SABC television studios in Auckland Park.

I want to try a new song, Tau ea Khale. You don't mind if I sit on your stoep and practise there?

What part of this-is-your-home don't you understand, you offspring of a witch? asked the old man.

He yelled for his eyes to take my chair to the stoep and asked someone else whose name I did not catch, but who turned out to be a daughter-in-law, to bring me a bowl of motoho fermented porridge – which surprised me; they ate as if they were still in a Lesotho village.

Soon Mabalane Street in front of Tau ea Khale's house was crowded with people of all ages dancing to my accordion as I tried out various tunes that would accompany the new hymn that was sparked by Tau ea Khale's words.

It was going to be makhele – lifela throughout, accompanied by accordion and drums. No chorus. No masholu. Since the hymn may be sung by more than one person, I would challenge Maleshoane to respond with her own hymn. If she was not able to compose one, I would compose it for her at the rehearsal tomorrow. Mohalalitoe and Mochini would not like it. I knew that already. Even now they were saying that Maleshoane was becoming too big for her boots in the band even though she was just a dancer. She strutted around, they said, as if she owned the band just because she was sleeping with the kheleke.

Oh yes, they were calling me a kheleke already.

And the people danced.

*

When I don't say anything, it doesn't mean I don't feel anything. Even a boy-child, he whose body has been allocated as food for the vultures, even a boy-child bleeds in the heart. You forget your cruel words, but they stay with me. The doer may forget, but the one who suffers the action remembers always. Every time I see you, my mind recalls your insults. No matter how hard I try to erase them, they are as stubborn as the writing of an indelible pencil. The purple eyesore that stays on paper to the end of the paper's days.

Ao-oelele-eeee seoeleoelele, even a muscular man like me feels the pain. Even a six-pack, hard as granite, pecs rippling like waves on a pool when you throw a stone, bleed when carved with a machete.

Ao-ooelele, the axe will forget that it chopped the tree, but the tree will always remember.

Ao-oelele-eeee, I, brother of Moliehi, boy-child whose songs shall live long after I am gone, I pray to you, grandmother in your grave, to come and vouch for me. I, whose chief is famous for his handsomeness and generosity, Chief Leshoboro Seeiso, the Principal Chief of Likhoele, I, a beautiful child among nations, I can cry tears of pain, can bleed blood that is red. Jooo nnaaa oeee!

I raised my purple blanket like wings ready to take off. The purple blanket with ornamental maize on the cob designs. Purple was the colour Mohalalitoe adopted. I spread my wings and a fan, hidden from the SABC television cameras, blew the blanket so that I seemed to be in flight. My Basotho hat, the mokorotlo grass hat, sat on the side of my head as if it were full of braggadocio. My accordion wailed like a lost child. An orphaned child. At times it sounded like a kolia-malla – a song of lament – yet one full of the kind of energy that forced the feet to jit-and-jive on the floor. After all, we do dance in the midst of death. We commemorate the dead with song and dance. I might as well commemorate a broken heart in a similar manner.

It was in that spirit that the five dancers, led by Maleshoane, performed their gyrations behind me. It was in that spirit Mochini-oa-Ipommpa beat the drums so vigorously I could smell hot rubber and feared the drumhead might burst. Or catch fire.

You would not have believed that was the same Mochini who agreed with Mohalalitoe, the man, when he attacked this song. It was a song of weaklings and not warriors, he said. Mochini agreed and added that perhaps it was a mistake to invite me to be a member of this outfit. Men of the Cult of Mohalalitoe did not cry or bleed like women. I should be composing boastful hymns about our prowess on the field of battle, about our fearlessness, about our readiness to fuck the Train or the Black Letlama or the Red Letlama at the slightest provocation. We ourselves needed to be provocative so that these older and more established groups could not ignore us. Our songs must be full of arrogance. On the stage our dance movements must show even at a glance that we are full of shit.

But I had made it clear right from the beginning that I would compose only the kind of hymns I would like to sing. Hymns that spoke of who I was deep down in my bones. Mohalalitoe, the man, was himself an accordionist and a hymn singer. If he wanted belligerent hymns, he was free to sing them. I could even back him with a second accordion if he asked nicely. But I would not – perhaps could not even if I tried – compose songs that disparaged or threatened others.

When we rehearsed, Mochini-oa-Ipommpa had only joined us sulkily. He kept on stealing a glance at Mohalalitoe, as if he were ashamed of being caught drumming for this shitty song. But after a few bars my accordion grabbed him by the nape. He stopped paying attention to Mohalalitoe and focused on his drum and on the dancers. Mohalalitoe was enthralled despite himself. The dancers were raising dust with their moves. Of course, only proverbial dust because we were in a glistening television studio.

When I turned around from my flight and faced the cameras, I changed the register of my hymn. I strained my eyes to see where Tau ea Khale was sitting in the small studio audience. I had invited him precisely for this moment, so that he could hear how I had turned words stolen from his lips into a hymn of the wanderers. Balelere le maloabe. Wanderers and vagabonds.

Ao-oelele-eeee! When I don't say anything, it doesn't mean I don't feel anything. Ao-oelele-eeee! Boy-child, Ngoan'a moshanyana kabela manong! Boy-child, he who will be shared by the vultures. I learn things from blind old men. Even things of the flesh. Fathers and grandfathers question my bachelorhood. Grandmothers want to know when I will gift them with grandchildren to spoil. I tell them as long as I am a wanderer, a travelling minstrel, I will not offend my ancestors by taking a wife. I will not waste my father's cattle by marrying someone's daughter. I don't want to marry for the walls of my father's house. I do not want loafers and dandies to eat my father's cattle while I am singing hymns in distant towns. While I am wandering in the wilderness with rain hitting hard on my skin.

All the while Maleshoane was circling me in a dance that challenged me to a duel. I jumped out of the imaginary circle and danced on a new spot. She leapt onto my space and encircled me once more in an aggressive dance. When I put a full stop on my hymn by stamping my feet in mock indignation, she came in with her response, singing the hymn better than we had rehearsed it.

Seoelele-oelele oeee, boy-child, since when do men fear a thing that has been eaten by other men? Since when do they despise masalla? Leftovers? Leave cowardice alone, boy-child. My father's kraal is waiting for your father's cattle. I am ready. I am waiting. Put me behind your father's door. And then leave for your wanderings. You were born for the road, brother of Moliehi. Let your hymns take you into the wilderness. Bo-mahlalela, the loafers, will knock at my door in the middle of the night. It is the story of today and a story of yesteryear. It is the story of our mothers and our grandmothers. Loafers and dandy boys always knock when real men are digging White man's gold from the belly of the earth. They won't finish it, boy-child.

See how heavy I am, child of Likhoele? See how well fed I am? This woman can never be finished by any loafer. When you return from your wanderings the thing will still be there, rato la ka, love of mine. It will still be intact. It never gets finished. Jo nna mme oeeeee!

An explosion of laughter and cheers!

Seoelele-oelele oeee, I am asking you, boy-child, what kind of boy are you who does not want to share with other children? Our elders say a delicious thing must be shared. The people shall share. This thing that will not get finished, why are you afraid to share it with others? Why are you so stingy to this nation of Moshoeshoe, boy-child? Why are you jealous of my generosity to this wonderful nation of blanket-wearers? Ma-apara kobo a matle? Jo nna mme oeeeee!

More and prolonged laughter and cheers. I couldn't help but laugh as well. I was tickled by her ingenuity. Those last lines about my not wanting to share and being stingy were not part of the rehearsal. They were not part of the hymn as we had devised it. She must have composed them spontaneously due to the chemistry she was having with the audience. Here we had a hymn singer in the making. One day she would be the new Mme Mpuse.

Maleshoane was fuelled by the plaudits, which included my laughter. She was throwing her copious weight around as if she owned that stage. As if she owned the accordionist and the drummer. As if she owned the rest of the dancers, who also retaliated in kind. As if she owned the host, Bhodloza, the camera people, the lights, the walls, everything. Her ownership of us all fuelled my accordion, and in return I co-owned all that I surveyed.

*

Mohalalitoe – the Cult of the Arum-Lily, that is – was playing with the big guns. People were talking of it in the same breath as

127

Letlama and the Cult of the Train. I thought it was all thanks to my song 'U Ka Se Nqete', which was getting a lot of airplay on many SABC radio stations, but particularly on Lesedi FM which was a Sesotho-language channel. In Lesotho too, MoAfrika FM and Radio Lesotho played it all the time because people demanded it on request programmes.

At first, I worried that the SABC would ban it because it was a bit naughty, especially the part that was sung by Maleshoane. After all, this was the same broadcaster that banned The Beatles after one of them claimed the band was more popular than Jesus Christ. It was in the olden days when the Boers were still the rulers, so obviously things had changed since then.

None of the DJs even commented on content. They just played the music and people went crazy.

Mohalalitoe, the man, and his sidekick, Mochini-oa-Ipommpa, hated 'U Ka Se Nqete'. Initially, that is. They said it was misrepresenting the Mohalalitoe brand. It was not manly. It was wimpy. It destroyed all of Mohalalitoe's branding plans. I didn't even know we had branding plans, or what branding plans were, but Mohalalitoe had them all worked out in his head. The band, or the whole movement, was named after a flower. Yet it was going to sing hymns that were full of arrogance and anger. Its masholu chorus singers would dance with sticks, pickaxes, spades and shovels raised threateningly. The band would have nothing to do with women choruses and women dancers. The men of the Cult of the Arum-Lily would be known for aggression. They would be feared even more than Letlama, more than the worst of the Train, more than the hymn singer who named himself after the coffin, Lekase. That would be the unique selling point of the group – named after a flower yet deadlier than a masumu snake. An unsettling contradiction.

My singing songs of weaklings, whose hearts were bleeding because of women, was working against that branding, as was my insistence on female dancers, and now on a female hymn singer in the form of Maleshoane. There would no longer be a contradiction. No one would marvel at the play between war and a flower. Instead people would say, no wonder they sing of womanish things, they are named after a flower!

Mohalalitoe had explained this philosophy to me immediately after the taping at the SABC television studios. He and Mochini were at pains to sit me down at Tau ea Khale's house in Senaoane to explain everything about branding, which I didn't give a damn about. In my view people should just be happy and sing. That's how it's always been for us wanderers. All this branding nonsense, this plotting and planning, this skulduggery, I felt, was something that was introduced by promoters and record companies to take the joy out of our carefree music.

Singing was a business, Mohalalitoe said. It was not something you just did for joy. I needed to learn to be more professional. Professionalism was what had made all the other bands successful. His point did make sense and after he and Mochini had left, and after Tau ea Khale had finished praising us for our wonderful performance and for stealing his words that he did not even remember uttering, I told Maleshoane that perhaps we should pay more attention to Mohalalitoe since he knew what was good for the Cult of the Arum-Lily. After all, he was the one who was able to get us a contract to cut a CD. He also arranged the videotaping at the SABC. He knew what he was doing.

I will stop frustrating his efforts, I said.

So, you will fire us? Maleshoane asked.

Why would I do that?

Part of Mohalalitoe's branding is that he doesn't want women, let alone a female hymn singer, she said. So you'll have to fire me and the dancers.

I could not answer that. I could not see it happening. There must be some way of being warlike without excluding women. Women could be warlike too. Mme Mpuse was a woman of the gun in her day. I had repeated that so many times to these men of the Cult of the Arum-Lily. But they seemed to be deaf to it.

Everything changed when 'U Ka Se Nqete' became popular. Mohalalitoe, the band, was on the tongue of everyone. Mohalalitoe, the man, was happy that we were selling thousands of records, which would translate into good royalties even after the record company was done with robbing us. Women particularly loved the song. Even at concerts when I played that one, they said they loved a man who was vulnerable. A man who could feel the pain. And acknowledge it.

Though Mohalalitoe, the man, was enjoying the fame my song had brought us, at drinking places he mocked me and said men despised my song. They were saying it was because I never went to the school of the mountain that I sang about things of love. I was never initiated into manhood, had never been circumcised. A man shouldn't be in the business of being hurt by women, and then announce that in a hymn. Women should be hurt by him, not the other way round. Women were the ones who should sing of a broken heart. Never mind a bleeding one.

A man shouldn't tolerate being told what Maleshoane was telling me on the stage in our performance.

It was only a song, I told him. And at concerts both men and women loved it. Men laughed the loudest. Even those who came from the gold mines of Welkom, from digging White man's gold from the belly of the earth, played the song on their tape recorders in buses and minibus taxis that were taking them to Lesotho to see the wives and children they had missed for months. They loved the way boy-child was such a self-deprecating musician. Some even said so in so many words, that this boy-child was a breath of fresh air.

I began the task of grooming Maleshoane into a hymn singer. I did it secretly when Mohalalitoe or Mochini were not present. She had the flair. After all, she had been dancing for hymn singers most of her life. She had an impish turn of phrase as well. Sometimes cheeky, sometimes coquettish. Therefore, she would be able to compose self-deprecating hymns. Perhaps self-deprecation was the way to go. It was something we would have to sell to Mohalalitoe, but not so much to Mochini. I had concluded that the latter was a blind follower. If Mohalalitoe bought it, Mochini would buy it.

*

Every gang had its own ngaka, or traditional healer. Every hymn singer with a cult following must have one. Or a team of lingaka. I was introduced to ours – meaning the ngaka of the Cult of the Arum-Lily – at a disused gold mine near Krugersdorp. Disused and abandoned by mining companies, that is, but highly productive for zama-zama illegal mining operations.

I was with Tau ea Khale, who I brought along as a good-luck charm and adviser in the ways of MaRussia. I was his eyes this time because the grandson who worked as his usual eyes was at school in Mapetla. Maleshoane had remained in Soweto with the other dancers because Mohalalitoe and Mochini said this particular mine was not a place for women. I was surprised to see quite a few women at the informal settlements next to the mining operation heaps and furrows. Even in the corrugated-iron shack where we waited for the healer, a woman served us mageu – the fermented non-alcoholic maize beverage much loved as an effective thirst-quencher.

The ngaka was a scruffy man known as Matsetsela, which merely means traditional healer. He looked like a sehoapa, a piece of biltong well seasoned with a lot of salt and pepper. He smelled like one too. He carried his medicinal paraphernalia in two well-worn rock-rabbit bags that hung on his neck. Unlike most lingaka I had known, he didn't wear white beads on his head, neck or wrists. He didn't wear any strings of cowrie shells either. You would pass him in the street and think he was just a regular homeless guy. What surprised me most was that he was a Mosotho. Top musicians and zama-zama miners preferred traditional healers from Malawi and Venda who were reputed to have stronger magic than your garden variety Mosotho ngaka.

Matsetsela asked Tau ea Khale to wait outside; he did not want anyone else to be in the house when he was working on a client. Otherwise the medicine would be too shy to be potent. The mageu woman led Tau ea Khale outside the shack and gave him a tin drum to sit on. She joined him, and I could hear them laugh at some joke the old man had made.

I expected Matsetsela to throw bones of divination, but he was not that kind of doctor. He was not a diviner. His work was not to foretell the future, but to tiisa me, which meant to strengthen me so that I became the greatest of all hymn singers. So that I became invincible to the machinations of rivals. So that my music attracted more followers than any other musician. So that I acquired more courage to lead followers into war in defence of our music and our self-granted mining rights.

Matsetsela took out the sharp quill of an eagle and performed the phatsa ritual, making two incisions on my forehead and rubbing some black medicinal stuff into them which got mixed with my blood. He expressed his surprise that I did not have any old scars on my forehead.

My mother was a Santa woman of the Catholic Church, I said by way of explanation. She did not believe in the phatsa inoculation ritual.

And your father allowed her to come into his household with such unAfrican laws? asked Matsetsela.

She was a strong woman who wanted to bring us up in the church, I said. My father left everything in her hands while he spent all his time digging White man's gold. When I began to sing the hymns of the wanderers, lifela tsa liparola thota, she was disappointed in me.

My mother was the reason I never went to the mophato initiation school. But I did not say that to Matsetsela. There was no need to keep on reminding these people that I was never circumcised and therefore I was worthy of their contempt.

That doesn't explain why you don't have the scars I made on your men recently, said Matsetsela. You were not there?

Oh, you have already performed the phatsa ritual on Mochini and Mohalalitoe? I asked.

I doctored them a long time ago, soon after they left the Cult of the Train, said the ngaka. I am talking of your followers who went to kill a corpse at that funeral at Likhoele.

At first I was puzzled. Kill a corpse?

You think they could do such a brave act in the midst of government ministers, police and soldiers without my strengthening them first? asked Matsetsela.

That funeral! The funeral at which Toloki was saved by the grave. The men in purple blankets. The very purple blanket I was wearing as I underwent the phatsa ritual.

133

You seem surprised, said Matsetsela. You didn't know about this? Are you new in this Cult of the Arum-Lily?

The Cult of the Arum-Lily is itself new, and I am its kheleke, I said boastfully. I didn't want him to see that the discovery of Mohala-litoe's role in the killings had shaken me.

Yes, that is what is wonderful about you, Men of the Flower, said Matsetsela. You are new yet you have achieved so much. Your songs are number one, especially that one – here he giggled – what is it called now? Yes, that one called 'U Ka Se Nqete'.

Though he was praising my song, I wished he would just shut up. The thought of Mohalalitoe and Mochini planning and carrying out such a dastardly act in my village sickened me. The villagers who died at that funeral were well known to me. Though the dead man whose corpse was riddled with bullets was not someone I knew personally since he went to the City of Gold when I was still a herdboy, only to return as a corpse, I knew his family. Though Likhoele is a big village, some might call it a peri-urban area, we all knew one another. What would my people say when they heard that I belonged to the group that caused such havoc in the village?

And now there was this new term of endearment for our murderous group: Men of the Flower!

You have now captured this mine, said the ngaka. It is all because of your brilliant leaders, Mohalalitoe and Mochini. I knew them when they were still with the Cult of the Train. I used to be one of the lingaka of the Cult of the Train. That's where your leaders stole me.

They are not my leaders, I said. We are all leaders. Remember I am the kheleke – the eloquent one – of the Cult of the Arum-Lily.

Yes, in all the other groups the kheleke is the leader of everything, including war. But from what I have noticed the real brains behind the success of your group is Mohalalitoe. And Mochini. Don't forget Mochini when it comes to mining.

I was learning so many new things about my own group; I was totally shaken.

After Matsetsela left, the mageu woman came with a plate piled with pap and chunks of meat. Mohalalitoe and Mochini returned and were also served pap and meat. And then she took another plate to Tau ea Khale outside.

Ngaka Matsetsela did a good job on you, said Mochini looking at the two inoculation incisions on my forehead.

Now we can introduce him to the miners as our kheleke, said Mohalalitoe.

Oh no, not yet, said Mochini. Miners must only meet the two of us, at least for now. This boy-child does not know how to project power.

Mohalalitoe nodded in agreement. Suddenly, Mochini had come into his own and was calling the shots?

He is talking shit when he says I cannot project power, I said. Anyway, why should I project power? I am a singer of hymns. Why would Mochini's word matter anyway?

When we talk about songs and hymns your word is important, said Mohalalitoe. But when we talk about the things of the mines Mochini-oa-Ipommpa is the expert.

And you? I asked. You are the expert of what? Of brutality? Of atrocity?

Calm down, man. Has Matsetsela's medicine made you mad? That was Mochini. He was staring down at me, chewing the rubbery meat with an open mouth to my face, making deliberate sounds of a man wearing gumboots walking in deep mud. I shifted on the bench and faced Mohalalitoe directly.

I know you are the one who shot bullets into the dead man's coffin at the funeral in my village, I said.

We, not only me, we of the Cult of the Arum-Lily, killed the dead man, said Mohalalitoe. You, me, Mochini, everyone else who identifies with the purple blanket. It was our first act of war. An act that taught everyone that Men of the Flower are ruthless. You cannot escape from them even if you die. They are so ruthless that they can even dig you out of your grave and kill you again.

Say it plainly, Mohalalitoe. You sent those killers?

Yes, I sent those people you call killers. I sent them to avenge our people. I sent them to establish my reputation. To leave a signature. To show off my brutality. I say *my* because you don't want to be associated with greatness. Otherwise, it's our brutality. I am quite willing to share it with the rest of my team-mates. Our brutality. The brutality of the Flower.

You have blood on your hands! I screamed. I was becoming hysterical. Some of my innocent neighbours died there.

Your hands are just as bloody, said the man calmly. You are as much of Mohalalitoe as I am.

We would not have got this mine if we had not killed the dead man in Likhoele, said Mochini.

We even own a mine, I said mockingly. Am I part of that as well?

On our way back to Johannesburg in Mohalalitoe's Mercedes-Benz, he began to explain how the mine was acquired.

They didn't mind talking about these things in the presence of Tau ea Khale after Mochini joked, He is blind, he can't sell us out.

Tau ea Khale responded, You offspring of Diablo, I have more insight than you sighted ones. I could sell you out for a penny, despite my blindness. But I am a man and have been to the mountain. I know koma, the secret song of the mountain, as well as any man who has been there. Plus, I didn't spend ten years at Sun City only to be an impimpi yamaBhunu – the snitch of the Boers. Plus, this boy-child is the son of my dead friend. Even if I were inclined to sell you – a very appetising thought – I would not sell him. He is part of you; to sell you out would be to sell him out too.

I hear you, Tau ea Khale, said Mohalalitoe, laughing and obviously liking the old man. But we are no longer ruled by the Boers. We are ruled by Mandela's people.

What is the difference? asked Tau ea Khale. Are we not still hungry?

Not any more, said Mochini, laughing. Not us Men of the Flower. We have now cornered a gold mine and our music will soon be minting it when royalties are paid.

I am more interested in how you got a mine by killing a dead man in my village in faraway Lesotho, I said, getting irritated by the digression.

First, the two men gave me a lesson on how gangs led by musicians got to own mines. These were mines that were abandoned by the multinational mining companies. Or were undergoing liquidation. Individual independent miners, mostly from neighbouring countries, but also from such South African provinces as the Eastern Cape, flocked into these mines to mine gold for themselves. Powerful gangs established their own rule over the mining communities and controlled everything. They taxed these artisan miners for a portion of any gold they harvested from the rocks inside the dangerous shafts. At other mines, depending on the gangs that ruled them, they charged miners a fee for going into the shaft and another fee for coming out. Since these miners spent weeks or even months underground, the gangs charged them exorbitant prices for the food that spaza traders sent down the shafts, and part of that profit was shared with the gang leaders. Any artisan miner who refused to pay protection fees was likely to be found dead in some mineshaft. And of course these mining activities were illegal, and therefore the miners could not resort to the law. The police turned a blind eye because many of them were on the payroll of the gang leaders.

Many of the Basotho hymn singers led gangs that had mines under their control. Sometimes they fought among themselves for territorial control – continuing the tradition of MaRussia of old.

But we had no time for that, said Mochini, displaying his knowledge of the finer points of illegal mining. We heard of this mine in Krugersdorp that was dominated mostly by Mozambican artisan miners. I decided we had to take it over.

The man whose corpse was riddled with bullets stood in Mochini's way. The man was a lackey of the Cult of the Train and wanted to enhance his stature by extending their influence from the mines of Welkom where they dominated to Krugersdorp and Randfontein. He was playing with fire because Mochini and Mohalalitoe had made up their minds that the specific mine in Krugersdorp would belong only to the Cult of the Arum-Lily.

He frustrated every move of mine, said Mochini. I sent out word that the Cult of Mohalalitoe was gunning for him. I had my young men, recently graduated from a mophato in Matelile, looking for him everywhere. Word spread that he was dead meat because the new boys in town, the Men of the Flower, were gunning for him. Very few people had heard of us then.

While we were actively looking for the man, Mohalalitoe chipped in, he was actively organising against us, sending spies to follow Mochini-oa-Ipommpa. We had to get him before he could get us. Unfortunately, others got to him before we did. I suspect it was his own gang. I suspect he was trying to establish himself independently of his Cult. We were not going to let things go just because his mates

138

killed him before we could do it. That gave us the opportunity to demonstrate to one and all that you do not mess with the Flower, for it will get you one way or the other. Not even death will save you.

Within days of the funeral shooting, the squatter settlement around the mine was infested with men in purple blankets. They were reputed to be carrying guns under their blankets that were bigger than those of the police. They closed the whole place down – shooting anyone who showed the slightest defiance, robbing small businesses such as spaza shops and butcheries, and raping women at will.

The security guards who had been left to guard the plant by the mining company that originally owned the mine before it went into liquidation took to their heels. Mohalalitoe shifted the focus. Whereas other gangs made money by taxing the miners and sharing their profits, Mohalalitoe focused on stripping the plant and selling everything that was metal.

One of the leading players in all this process was the ngaka, Matsetsela, who had a reputation already from his days with the Cult of the Train. Fearful miners and their families at the squatter camp believed that under their purple blankets not only did the Men of the Flower hide their machine guns, but the blankets themselves protected them from bullets. Thanks to the potent medicine of Matsetsela, bullets could not penetrate those blankets. Enemies did not fight back but took to their heels when the men in pherese, which is Sesotho for purple, approached singing their masholu.

After the Mercedes-Benz dropped us in Senaoane, Tau ea Khale whispered to me before we entered the house: I can see what you learned today has upset you.

I am supposed to be one of them, but they left me out of all these things, I said.

Is that what is really upsetting you?

139

He was blind but he could see through me.

Those partners of yours are brave men. They remind me of the true MaRussia of my day. They remind me of myself before prison tamed me. But you, you were not made for this.

Are you suggesting I am weak? I asked, showing that I was truly offended. I am not man enough?

Oh, no, said Tau ea Khale. You are more than man enough. You are not weak either. You are a very strong man. But your strength may be made for other things. I don't know. I can only say what I observe. You know best.

You sound as if you think I should withdraw from the Cult of the Arum-Lily.

Who am I even to suggest what road you should take? You know best what your spirit wants.

*

Cow, go back home, you're old.

It was a saying that the elders used when you had been gone from home for too long. To be fair to cows, it applied to bulls and oxen as well, as cow in this case was not gendered. After a few months I followed that advice and Maleshoane and I went to Likhoele. We were performing in the mining towns of the Free State and had a week between performances. Mohalalitoe dropped us at my father's homestead and proceeded to his own village in Thabana Morena.

The first person I looked for was Toloki. I wanted to give him back his accordion or its price. I was hoping he would agree to take the money because my fingers were now used to his accordion. It had come to know me so well and could hear my thoughts. It responded to my brain even before my fingers could press the buttons and the keys. It seemed my soul and its soul were entwined.

140

Toloki was not in the mokhoro. His bedding was not there either.

Moliehi was not in the main house. Nor was Noria. Perhaps Toloki left with his Noria. Perhaps there was a reconciliation and they were now mourning their hearts out across the oceans. But what about Moliehi, child of my mother? Where could she be?

Maleshoane said I should not worry, Moliehi was a big girl. And then she busied herself with cleaning up my hut. A lot of dust had accumulated in the weeks that we were away. Even the clearing in front of the houses had not been swept for quite some time. Weeds were beginning to grow among the stones that made up the high stoep and in the cracks of the stoep itself. It was like no one lived there any more.

For the first time in weeks we had an early night. The skin hungered for another skin. Blood cried for another blood.

Deep in the night Shoane whispered, You are not yourself. What is eating you?

I don't know, I said. Perhaps Moliehi.

No. It is not that. You have not been yourself for weeks. Since you returned from that mine in Krugersdorp, she said.

I want to leave Mohalalitoe, I said.

You want to kick him out of the band, you mean?

I mean leave the Cult of Mohalalitoe, not Mohalalitoe the man. I miss my freedom.

Maleshoane grabbed me by my naked shoulders and shook them in disbelief.

You want to leave an arrangement that has put so much bread on our table, with so much thick butter on both sides to boot? You miss your ways of boloabe, of wandering from village to village playing at skanky good-time places? Are you mad? This outfit gave me the opportunity to be a hymn singer when everyone thought I was just a dancer.

I gave you that opportunity in my very madness, I said. Are you forgetting that both Mohalalitoe and Mochini objected?

You were doing something for your lover, to pay back for my love handles that were bruised because of your rough ways. Yes, you gave me that opportunity ... in their band.

Our band. It is mine too. We are all equal partners.

Nobody told me I am an equal partner, said Shoane.

Of course you are not. There are three equal partners in Mohalalitoe: it is me, Mochini and Mohalalitoe. So, don't tella me, I added, meaning she should stop looking down on me.

Whatever your problem is, I am not going to allow you to leave the Cult of the Arum-Lily. Many big things are still going to happen for you. You told me you have never had so much money before. And there is more to come. People love your songs. They love mine too, which are really your songs since they come from your composition. Well, I do add salt and pepper and a little bit of Rajah curry powder, but most of the words are yours. Most of the anguish, at least.

She was still talking when I drifted into sleep.

At dawn we were woken by the voices of two drunken women shouting out what they imagined was a song. Whatever it was, it was out of tune.

That's your sister and her lover, said Maleshoane.

Of course, she was making a mistake. Sister, yes, but she couldn't have been with a lover. There were two women singing, not a man and a woman.

It was midday before Moliehi and Noria walked out of the main house. Shoane and I joined them on the stoep.

What happened to you? I asked. Where were you?

We went to make ourselves happy, said Noria, though I had not directed the question to her.

142

This was obviously a new Moliehi. The Moliehi who went to good-time places to make herself happy.

Where is Toloki? I asked.

He left, but not for good yet, said Moliehi. He went to mourn at various places to accumulate enough money to go overseas.

I have the money for him, I said. More than just for the accordion. I have as much money as he needs for his ticket, for his mofao provisions, for his needs where he is going.

So, you are rich now? asked Moliehi mockingly.

Not rich, but we have enough, I said.

We have heard of your liqi in Gauteng, said Noria. Everybody is singing your naughty song. Even children.

I will have enough money to look after you, child of my mother, I said. You have looked after us when I was a leloabe. From now on you will want for nothing for the rest of your life.

Provided you don't do something stupid and leave the band that is still going to make you more money, said Maleshoane. Only a fool slaughters a cow that bears so many calves and gives so much milk.

I do not want to be looked after, child of my mother, said Moliehi. I want to look after myself. I have the same gifts as you have.

Don't tell me you still want to be a famo dancer, I said.

No, said Noria emphatically. She wants to be a singer now. And she can do it.

I burst out laughing, which infuriated Noria and Moliehi and amused Maleshoane.

Am I going to die with all these songs that are swelling in my heart? asked Moliehi.

Songs? You? I asked and burst out laughing again.

If I cannot be a dancer then I want to be a singer, said Moliehi.

She was serious. Laughter died on my lips. I was becoming exasperated.

You are my sister, child of my mother, I said. It is tough out there. It is not as glamorous as you hear us sing on Radio Lesotho and Lesedi FM or see us on television. It is a dirty world out there. I want you to keep your cleanliness. I place you on a pedestal.

When Maleshoane butted in I knew she was going to undermine everything I was trying to do here. And she did.

Never allow any man to put you on a pedestal, she said. A pedestal is a prison.

I am trying to protect my sister here, I said, losing my temper. What are you trying to do?

You have always protected me, child of my mother, said Moliehi. Oh, child of my mother shouldn't touch this or that! Oh, child of my mother is brittle, she will break! Oh, child of my mother shouldn't climb trees and swing in them like a boy! In the meantime, I was the one who was working in the fields, bringing home the harvest. The bags of maize and beans in that mokhoro are from these hands. Now you don't want me to sing because you are protecting me?

Tell him what we did to a man who tried to rape you last night, said Noria.

It is our business what we did last night, said Moliehi.

Well, we beat him up, said Noria. We beat him to a pulp. We left him there for dead. Don't be surprised if you see police coming for us before the end of this day.

7

Bones

The road was gruelling, thanks to 'U Ka Se Nqete'. I shouldn't have composed that song. It would be the death of me, though one would be ungrateful to complain. It was the one they demanded all the time. Over and over. Ingoma emnandi iyaphindwa, they said in the language of Gauteng. A great song must be repeated. Over and over again. Though I was tired of it and was keen to focus on new songs that were crying to be sung, burning my insides, wanting to burst out, Maleshoane was having the time of her life. Every night on the stage she climbed more and more steps. O hloa litepe. To higher realms of performance. And of improvisation.

Sometimes I thought she was getting carried away. Becoming too explicit. Every time she came with something new right there on stage, something we had not rehearsed before, she looked at me with a twinkle in her eye. I smiled back to say way to go. But when I thought she was going beyond the bounds of propriety I shook my head and made a funny face to say, wow, wait a minute. Take it easy, woman of Leribe. Woman of Hlotse Mankoaneng where they boast of the best shebeens in the district. Mind your tongue, there may be pastors in the house. Deacons, bishops and popes. The road to hell is paved with the sweet-talking decadence of a kheleke.

Whenever she did her shiqi shiqi thing, throwing her weight about, causing earth tremors as her feet stamped on the stage, threatening to strip naked right there in the public arena, with audiences clapping their hands and encouraging her to do it, she reminded me of one particular day in the week that we spent at Likhoele almost a year ago. Yes, it was all of eleven-and-something months since we left my village after organising a big feast to thank the ancestors.

The whole village had gathered at the clearing in front of Moliehi's house, spreading to the rocks that used to be the corral, eating the ox and the goat that I had slaughtered and drinking the sorghum beer that Moliehi, Noria and Maleshoane had brewed.

I am sure the ancestors were shocked out of their wits because I had never made a feast in their honour. It was not out of disrespect or that I did not recognise them as a man brought up by a Christian woman of the Catholic Church. Basotho Christians of all faiths generally venerate ancestors and slaughter beasts for them, despite the objection of White missionaries. Truly, people continue to believe in the God and Jesus of Christian churches, and still talk to their ancestors. It was important that I talked to mine too, now that I had the means. It was important that I thanked them that I was finally referred to as a kheleke, the eloquent one – a title one was given by followers, by radio and television hosts and even by rivals. I have not heard rivals call me that, though. I have not heard them even obliquely insulting me or threatening me with likobiso, the coded words that did not mention one's name directly but were framed in such a way that everyone knew they were referring to one. One day that would happen too. Only then would I be a true kheleke. Only then would I feel in my heart, in my blood, in my bones that I was the eloquent one.

Definitely things had changed for the better for me even financially, though Maleshoane kept on reminding me that I was being robbed blind by Mohalalitoe and his sidekick Mochini-oa-Ipommpa.

Did you see how full the hall was? Maleshoane would ask. And you agree to be paid such a pittance? You know where all the money goes? To Mohalalitoe.

Yes, I said. We are working to build Mohalalitoe into a formidable organisation.

I am talking of Mohalalitoe the man, said Maleshoane. I am not talking of the Cult of the Arum-Lily but of Mohalalitoe, the bastard man. All the money goes into his pocket. That's why he drives a Mercedes-Benz and you have no car.

I, on the other hand, was just happy to have money. I had never had so much money in my life. Hence the feast to thank the ancestors.

Normally some of the ritual would have happened at my father's grave. But he had no grave in the village. His grave was five hundred metres deep in some Johannesburg gold mine known as Durban Deep, according to what Tau ea Khale discovered. So, my mother's grave served the purpose. I visited it early that morning, surrounded by uncles both from my mother's and father's sides, and led by Moliehi, child of my mother. I swore on that grave in the presence of all those relatives that I would find my father's bones if it were the last thing I did and give them a dignified burial next to her grave in the village of Likhoele.

That would seal the good fortune I was currently enjoying. And more would flow from the ancestral realm into my pocket, and even more into my bank account. Later in life, when I was ready to return to my village to rebuild my father's homestead, more would flow into my father's corral to replace the cattle that were lost through my carelessness while I pursued the song.

From the grave we washed our hands in aloe vera water and variously joined in the busy-ness of the event. I got my korostina just to create some nostalgia for those who remembered me during the days of the concertina.

Maleshoane started dancing and freestyling a hymn. It was just a lot of snippets from hymns and proverbs that didn't amount to anything coherent. But people didn't mind. They were more focused on her dance and were loving it. Shiqi shiqi. She was throwing her weight around, stamping on the ground, shaking her ample bottom and her ample breasts, to the rhythm of the concertina. I noticed that Moliehi, child of my mother, had improvised percussion with a saucepan and a spoon. She was beating the utensils to the rhythm of my concertina and Maleshoane's stamping while dancing in place on the sidelines. Maleshoane beckoned her to come join her in the arena, but she shook her head shyly. I snickered to myself; this was a woman who expressed aspirations of being, first, a dancer, and of late a singer of hymns. And here she was shy to perform in front of fellow villagers who knew her from the time she was a baby. And yet she thought she could do it in front of merciless strangers?

Ha ke rata nka tsola, yelled Maleshoane in the midst of a scintillating concertina. She was threatening to strip naked.

Tsola! Tsola! Tsola! The people were chanting. Strip naked! Strip naked! Strip naked!

She took off her blouse and waved it around as she danced. Her bosom, restrained by a pink double-D brassiere, was bobbing and heaving to the concertina and percussion. She threw the blouse in Noria's direction, who caught it. Maleshoane teased around,

148

pretending she was going to take off her skirt. People chanted even louder that she should go ahead and strip.

What are you showing the children, you heathens? said a man as he left in disgust.

A woman who heard him laughed and said, You came to the wrong place, old man. These are singers of the hymns of wanderers. They are not ruled by inhibitions.

When people finally realised that Maleshoane had no intention of stripping they lost interest in her and demanded that I play 'U Ka Se Nqete'. I had only played a few bars when a truck loaded with men in purple blankets stopped at the gate. Mohalalitoe and Mochini stepped down. I had told them of the feast, and they had said they would not attend as they had to acquire another mine in the Free State, a well-known territory of the Cult of the Train. I had not invited all these men of the Cult of the Arum-Lily. But in Sesotho a feast was for everyone. Not only those who had been notified. Notified, not invited. You merely told people that on such and such a day you would slaughter for the ancestors and they came. Some got it from the grapevine and came. Men came early enough to help with the slaughter of the beasts and the cooking of those parts that were reserved by custom for men. Women came early to cut the vegetables and cooked for everyone else. Some had come days earlier to help with the brewing of sorghum beer, which took days to ferment properly.

The men in purple alighted and followed Mohalalitoe as he walked grandly towards the stoep where I was standing playing the concertina. He raised his hand and the music stopped.

Boy-child, boy-child, boy-child, you don't play our song at a timiti or famo party, he said.

Does this look like a famo party or timiti to you, Mohalalitoe? I asked. This is a feast in honour of those who are in the ground.

Yes, but that song is our meal ticket, you are cheapening it when you sing it at just any event where people are not paying to hear it. You are also cheapening yourself and the Cult of the Arum-Lily as a brand.

There came that brand thing again that had messed up my life.

I don't want to be a brand, I said. I just want to be a free man who can sing with his people any time he feels like it.

And you are not wearing your pherese, said Mohalalitoe as if talking to a schoolboy who had come to school without wearing his school uniform.

Pherese was the colour purple in Sesotho.

How will villagers identify you as a Man of the Flower if you don't wear your pherese? asked Mochini. How will they respect you?

I laughed and said, You guys have just come to mess up my feast.

This seemed to frustrate Mochini. He was always at a loss for words whenever he thought I was not taking important things seriously. Or was being impertinent. To them this brand thing was a matter of life and death.

I realised that the crowd was silent. The crowd had been silent from the time Mohalalitoe and his sidekick walked into the clearing in front of Moliehi's house. Even the boisterous Maleshoane was standing silently with Moliehi and Noria, her blouse now on.

Mohalalitoe seemed to enjoy the awkward silence he had brought. He started a song that sounded more like the mangae that the graduands of the initiation school of the mountain sang. The men in purple responded with a makhele-style chorus in two-part harmony – deep basso and sharp tenor. The resonance filled the air. Yet the women did not ululate as would have been the norm. I noticed that

150

the older ones were gradually peeling themselves from the crowd and walking away. Some older men did the same. The younger ones just stood there staring in awe at the men in purple.

After the song, just before he could start another one, I invited Mohalalitoe and Mochini to go into the main house, Moliehi's, so they could be served something to eat. I requested the men in purple to sit by the corral where they would be served their meat and beer.

Did you notice that? said Mohalalitoe as he chewed on the meat. People are dead scared of Mohalalitoe. Did you see how they were quivering when we entered?

And that's a good thing? I asked.

Of course! said Mochini.

What else can it be? asked Mohalalitoe. They remember us from that funeral where we shot the corpse to a second death. They remember the men in purple blankets. And they will tell others that they saw them with their own eyes at your feast. Now they know you are a Man of the Flower. They will respect you. Even rival bands will hear that we were here in flesh and blood, in this village of Likhoele, without fear or favour, and then they will see that we are devils incarnate.

People spoke about the feast for a long time. Or rather about the men in pherese at my feast. The men who sang and danced their way to the graveside at a funeral and pumped bullets into the coffin, and then caused mayhem by shooting randomly, killing and injuring innocent people.

My fellow villagers were shocked that I, boy-child, was part of the outfit that committed such atrocities. This boy-child whose father was an upright citizen who worked hard for his family and even died when the table fell on him in the mine. This boy-child whose mother was a Santa woman of the Catholic Church who prided

151

herself on her black-and-purple uniform. The very boy-child whose sister is Moliehi, the tough one who never misses a single letsema work-party in the village. This boy-child is now seen in the company of gangsters who terrorise innocent villagers.

These were older citizens, pillars of the community.

However, young men and women with bright impressionable eyes were in awe of me for belonging to such a warrior cult. I, boy-child, was being admired for something other than my song. I, boy-child, who could never harm even a bedbug after feeding on my blood! Boy-child, who would be devoured by the vultures only in his playful imagination. Only in swagger.

I just had to enjoy the attention and play along. Though I had threatened Maleshoane that I would resign from Mohalalitoe, I decided otherwise. At least for now. I just had to enjoy the glory first.

*

Tau ea Khale was the one who told me about Durban Deep. That's where my father worked and died. He got the information from those who used to work with him. Tau ea Khale was already serving his sentence at the time.

We had believed all the time that he worked in Johannesburg and died there, I said. I wonder why we were lied to when he was in Durban all that time.

No one lied to you. Durban Deep is not in Durban but in Johannesburg. In the Roodepoort municipality, in fact. It is less than thirty minutes from the CBD, said Tau ea Khale, referring to the downtown area officially known as the Central Business District.

Tau ea Khale introduced me to a man who insisted on remaining nameless. He would have remained faceless by keeping his balaclava on all the time if it were not going to be awkward in public. He hid his mouth under the old lesolanka blanket he was wearing, which muffled his voice when he spoke.

He worked with your father, said Tau ea Khale. He will take us to Durban Deep to show us the shaft where your father lies buried.

I would have expected him to look older if he worked with my father. Yes, he looked weather-beaten enough, but not as much as Tau ea Khale who I surmised was roughly my father's age.

If we go early enough, I'll be back in time for my show, I said.

We had the whole day, and the show at the Diepkloof Hall was going to start at seven-thirty. I did not tell anyone about this trip, not even Maleshoane. She had discouraged me from looking for my father, saying I should let resting bones rest. After all, the ancestors had continued to bless us with success in our music; we shouldn't upset the order of things as they stood. It was something very close to what Tau ea Khale once asked me. Why do you want to bother your father when he is having a wonderful time with his fellow ancestors? Why do you want to keep on reminding him that his bones are in a mine and not in a well-cared-for grave like those of his colleagues? I am sure by now in the hustle-bustle of the Afterlife he has forgotten where his bones are.

I have to do right by my father, Tau ea Khale. That was my final word.

I would be proud to have a son like you, he said.

After I had paid the nameless man his fee, we took a taxi to Durban Deep. I was Tau ea Khale's eyes this time as the boy was at school. I held his arm as we negotiated our way among the rubble, though he made things difficult for me by pulling away, clearly demonstrating that he trusted his white cane better than my guidance.

We plodded our way between shimmering hills of gold dust, past a rusty headgear. It was small wonder it still stood there, it being iron and all. Perhaps it was too heavy to be stripped for scrap metal. Maybe one day when the ground refused to yield any more gold and hunger struck, they'd find a way to melt all that metal.

The mine was abandoned ten years before by mining companies, but not by hundreds of people who established their homes in the shacks, built from scraps that used to roof some of the ruins, and in the rundown houses, most of which had corrugated iron for windows and doors. Most of the residents were descendants of miners who came from different countries in southern Africa, and now had no other home but this one.

The nameless one led us to a house which I later learned once belonged to a mine manager in the heydays of the mine who would, of course, by virtue of that position, have been a White man. Windows and doors were covered with plastic, Masonite boards and cardboard. A television was blaring inside, and a group of men sat on makeshift furniture of concrete blocks, beer crates and tin drums. They glared at us with glazed eyes that betrayed suspicion. They were puffing a zol of marijuana that was doing the rounds, from one man to the next. The room was filled with smoke, which nevertheless fizzled out through the many gaping holes in the walls and roof.

Wait right there, said a man in a letlama blanket.

He was the only one in a blanket. The rest were wearing dirty T-shirts and torn jeans. I wondered if the letlama was just an innocent attire that a proud Mosotho man would wear for its beauty or if it meant something deeper, such as that this mine was ruled by the Letlama musicians.

They have to smoke the dagga to embolden themselves before they go into the mine, said the nameless one. You might need to do likewise. It is scary down there, and very deep.

154

It is enough to know me only as Soalakahla, said the man in the letlama blanket. At least he was giving us a name to go by, unlike our guide who didn't even give us a pseudonym.

Who owns this mine? I asked, my curiosity getting the better of me.

Who wants to know? asked Soalakahla.

You are asking questions that are never asked by intelligent people, said the nameless one.

The blind man wants to go underground too? How is he going to see the gold? asked Soalakahla to the laughter of his dagga-smoking mates.

You offspring of Diablo, said Tau ea Khale, pointing his white cane in their direction, you'll be blind too one day, if you don't die before then. See if it will be something to joke about.

The men must have taken it as a curse because they quickly apologised and said Soalakahla was only playing.

We do not want to anger your grey hair, old man, said one man. We still want our ancestors to bless us.

You still remember which shaft it was? asked Soalakahla.

I will find it, said the nameless one. I know this mine inside out.

I paid Soalakahla his fee for allowing me and the nameless one into the shaft. Tau ea Khale would remain outside. He said he would wait for us at the entrance, however long we took.

We learned that each one of those miners who were fortifying themselves with pluck paid him seventy rands to enter a shaft and a hundred and fifty rands to get out. It didn't matter how much time they spent there. Most went with provisions to last them days. They came out with bags of rocks from which gold may or may not be found. If some gold was found, then a percentage of the money went to the gang. We were charged ten times the normal amount because we were not going to bring out any rocks, but were searching for dead people, as Soalakahla put it.

It was treacherous to manoeuvre our way down the shaft without any safety gear. There were no longer any cages, so we had to use ropes that we rented from Soalakahla to abseil our way down to a drop of almost four hundred metres, tying them on whatever frames remained, and hoping to God that they would still be strong enough to carry our weight. A number of tunnels branched off, which made it possible for us to take a rest, nibble on our provisions of biltong and potato crisps, and take a drink of water. I stopped the nameless one from smoking; what if there was deadly methane gas there?

It took us hours to get to the tunnel that the nameless man identified as the one they were working in when the table fell.

I wouldn't be doing this if my children were not starving, said the nameless man, and his voice echoed numerous times.

I understand, I responded with my own echoes.

It was as hot as hell as we negotiated the tunnel, using hand-held torches to find our way, sometimes having to wade through muddy water. Three pools of light told me that we were coming across a group of miners. There were indeed three of them, battery lamps on their helmets, chiselling the rock, and getting ready to insert a stick of dynamite.

What are you doing here, you men? This part of the tunnel is our turf, said one of the men.

They noticed that we were not wearing our lights on our helmets but were holding the torches with our hands. Therefore, we were not mining.

Who are you, what do you want? the man asked again. Are you from the law? If so, you will not get out of here alive.

The nameless one laughed and said, After threatening us with death do you think we would admit that we are from the law?

The men became a little bit more at ease. We could not be from the law. People from the law did not have any sense of humour.

This man's father was a miner here in the days of the White man, said the nameless one. We were working on this winze when the table fell. He died here and was never recovered. This man, a great kheleke of our time, is looking for his bones.

We come across skeletons of miners all the time down here, said one of the men. How will he know which one is his father?

That was one question I had considered but was encouraged when the nameless one told me that when the table fell at that particular spot, the only casualty was my father. He could not be rescued, and his body could not be recovered because the table that fell on him was really a container that dropped into a sinkhole, burying him. All we needed to do at that point was to find the container, and then next time I would return with experts who would cut through it and get my father out of there. But we didn't have time to explain all this to the men.

We'll know him, I said. Trust me, we'll know him.

You come at the wrong time, said the man. We have no time for conversation. We are about to insert dynamite here.

He was brandishing a stick of dynamite.

We have no time for conversation either, said the nameless one. Good luck with your mining.

As we walked away, one of the men called after us. Just around the corner over there, there are two women waiting for customers. You are free to help yourselves if you have the money.

We thought he was joking, chuckled a bit, and walked on.

You must not tell people I am a kheleke, I said to the nameless one.

It's a great thing. Are you ashamed of it?

You don't know if this mine belongs to rival musicians, I said, amazed at his stupidity. I want to come out of here alive.

As we slogged on our torches shone on what I believed were ghosts. At the same time there was a big explosion. I was so startled that I fell flat on my bottom in the water. The ghosts giggled.

It's just dynamite, said one of them.

It turned out there were two scantily dressed women sitting on a rock. Maybe five hundred metres under the ground, in the heat of hell. No wonder they were scantily dressed.

We are available for a quick one, said one of them.

You are miners too? I asked.

Yes, said the woman, but we don't mine gold. We mine men.

Trust a kheleke to ask a stupid question, said the nameless one. What part of being available for a quick one don't you understand?

We service them so that they get more strength to mine the gold, said the second one.

We are very cheap and are great at our job, said the first one. Try us.

We are good, thank you, said the nameless one as we moved on.

Maybe next time, I said, waving goodbye. It didn't matter if they could not see my hand in the dark, as our torches were only illuminating our path.

After we had trudged on for a distance that I believed was out of earshot, I said, In this dog-eat-dog world, I wonder how they survive in these dangerous tunnels that have not been maintained for a decade or more without being raped for free, without being robbed of their hard-earned cash, and without being murdered by some pervert.

Simple, said the nameless one. They must be owned by a feared pimp. Maybe the very same musicians who run the mine.

Another explosion, a distance away this time. The sound reverberated and the earth shook.

We had walked for more than five hours and were not getting to any place that the nameless one could identify as the spot where the container was buried.

It's all these dynamite explosions, he said. They have changed the map that I remembered in my head.

It was getting late and I feared for my concert.

It took us many hours to return to the surface, by which time it was already seven in the evening. I was worried because I didn't know where to find Tau ea Khale. He had said he would wait at the entrance, but I didn't expect him still to be there at that hour.

A boy came running.

You are looking for the old man? he asked, and without waiting for the response he continued, He is watching the women.

He can't watch anybody, said the nameless one. He's blind.

Come, I'll show you, said the boy.

We followed him through a maze of shacks and dilapidated mine houses, until we got to an open space where women were crushing stone with iron or granite pestles. And there was Tau ea Khale drinking beer from a plastic mug that used to be a container for snuff. He was nodding his head and tapping his foot in time to the song of the women.

The owners of each heap of stones were standing, eyes agog in anticipation of what their rocks would yield. Each took their crushed stone to yet another group of women who placed it in a tin drum that spun the stone mixed with mercury, and then they burnt the mercury off, leaving gold.

I stood watching for a while, fascinated by this whole process. I felt sorry for the many disappointed faces when the yield was only small amounts of gold, and in some cases nothing at all. The next day they would defy death once more in the infernal belly of the earth, and chisel the rock, and insert dynamite, and chisel once more, and break the stones, and put the promising ones in sacks to take back to the surface. Often this process took days or even weeks. That was why enterprising traders went down with essential goods such as bread, corned beef and cigarettes to sell at exorbitant prices to those miners who were determined to stay underground until they struck gold.

You said you had a concert tonight, said the nameless one.

I had panicked and was done with it as we worked our arduous way back to the surface. There was no way I would make Diepkloof Hall on time. It was almost eight.

Mohalalitoe and Mochini will play, I said. Maleshoane too.

Tau ea Khale's sharp ear heard my voice.

Son of my friend, you have returned, he said.

I walked to him.

We did not find the container, Tau ea Khale, I said. We'll try again another day.

Soalakahla arrived and came straight to me. He patted me on the shoulder and beckoned me to follow him. His face was stern, quite different from the Soalakahla of the morning when I paid him a lot of money. Without a word he stopped the nameless one who wanted to come along.

Where are we going? I asked as we walked away from the shacks to a dilapidated building that used to be a shop, as proclaimed by large letters on its face: Bob's Supermarket. Families lived there and had divided the interior into rooms. Soalakahla led me to one of the rooms where five men in letlama blankets sat drinking whisky.

When we heard there is a kheleke here we wondered, what kheleke? Only our group has people who can be called likheleke, said one of

160

the men, the fat one whose letlama was pinned on the front, woman-style. Basotho men pinned their blankets on the shoulder, particularly the left shoulder. He was sitting carelessly on a wooden chair, his T-shirt falling short of covering his bulging stomach.

The rest of the men, including Soalakahla, broke into laughter, and kept on repeating, kheleke? Who gave him that title? How come we have never heard of him? Kheleke? Khilik banna!

They were having a great time mocking me. I just stood there, waiting for them to finish their laughter.

You don't know how to talk? asked the fat man.

I talk when necessary. I talk on the stage, with either a koriana or a korostina in my hand. I talk better than any man here or anywhere else, I said, displaying the kind of bravado I had never known myself for. But once you disparage my eloquence, you have earned my disrespect. I am boy-child even in enemy territory. You remember how I stood my ground at the famo party back in Matelile months ago. My only hope was that I would not wake up in the hospital as I did then.

He is full of shit, said one man.

He is full of shit, agreed the fat man.

Soalakahla looked at me, and for the first time I saw admiration in his eyes.

What does he want here? said one man. That's what I want to know. What does a Mohalalitoe man want in our territory?

To steal it, said one man, just like they stole Krugersdorp. Just like they stole Randfontein.

You came to spy on us, didn't you? asked the fat man. Is your Cult of the Arum-Lily trying to take over this mine? Did they send you as a spy?

Do you think the Men of the Flower are so stupid that they would send their best kheleke as a spy? I asked. Wouldn't it be more intelligent for them to send a nonentity disguised as a miner to do that?

They didn't have an answer to that.

Didn't your lackey here, Soalakahla, tell you I am here to look for my father and nothing else? I added.

I am not a lackey, said Soalakahla looking at the fat man for defence.

You killed our man and then you come to our mine looking for your father? the fat man said instead.

I never killed anybody, I said. The very thought horrified me.

It was the men of Mohalalitoe who attacked the funeral of our man at Likhoele, said the fat man.

Ah, that funeral! It was in my village. From what I heard your man was killed by the Men of the Train, I said.

I was not sure here whether I was confusing issues. Was he of the Train, from what the rumours said in the village, or was he killed by the Cult of the Train? These men of Letlama were owning him now.

It doesn't matter who killed him first, said the fat man, obviously losing patience with the debate. The fact is men of Mohalalitoe killed him again when he was being given a decent burial. We shall not forget that. We are still planning our revenge. And it shall be public. It shall be spectacular. Our leaders are still fuming, though it was a year ago.

I was not part of that. I was playing with Puseletso Seema at the time. I only heard of Mohalalitoe's involvement a year after it had happened. I am against the wars of the musicians. I think we are all children of a man. We all need to get along.

The men agreed with me. They were so effusive in their yeah-yeahs and in nodding their heads that I suspected they were having me on. They were up to something.

You are a good man at heart, said the fat man. You just fell in with the wrong crowd. You should be with Letlama instead. With Letlama your music will reach the world. And, as you can see, you will have other opportunities too.

I knew he was talking of the money to be made in illegal mining. Everyone knew that Letlama had conquered the illegal mining operations in the whole of Gauteng and North West while the Cult of the Train was dominant in the Free State, with the main operations at the abandoned gold mines of Welkom. Letlama's source of anger was that the Cult of the Arum-Lily took over the mine in Krugersdorp, breaking their monopoly in a province they had hitherto controlled. Their anger was not only with Mohalalitoe, but with the police who allowed the takeover to happen. Mohalalitoe must have paid more money to buy them over to their side.

The police who ate our money and then took money from you cowards will pay the price, said the fat man.

He was no longer jovial. The rest of the men followed his mood. I knew that though he was a mere lieutenant of the real bosses of Letlama, the likheleke themselves, this was no idle threat. He was saying what they had talked about before, what the gang aimed to do to regain their lost dignity. Letlama was famous for brutality. They were so brutal that they killed policemen inside police stations.

We know you are supposed to be playing at Diepkloof Hall as we speak, said the fat man. And yet you are here with us. You really don't care for Mohalalitoe. They are only using you, from what I hear. Unlike all the likheleke I know, you don't have any power, you don't own the Cult of the Arum-Lily. Everything is owned by the man who stole the wings of Khosi Mosotho Chakela. You should be with us where you will have real power as a true kheleke.

As if he had noticed for the first time that I had been standing all along, he demanded that I be given a chair and a glass. As I took a sip of whisky, I thought about what he had just said, that I was being used. I thought I was using them to reach the heights of a recording star and be seen on television on a daily basis like the very same Mosotho Chakela of the Cult of the Train or the leaders of Letlama such as Lekase Coffin, Mahlanya and others.

The fat man was saying the same thing Maleshoane had once said. Actually, not once but many times after the show.

You abandoned your blind man, said a woman leading Tau ea Khale into the room.

You offspring of Diablo, said Tau ea Khale. I would be comfortably sleeping in my bed in Senaoane by now.

I apologise, Tau ea Khale, I said. I was ashamed of myself for not insisting that he be brought in. These men kidnapped me, and I had no way of getting back to you.

He is exaggerating, old man, said the fat one. Gentlemen like us cannot be kidnappers. We merely wanted to talk business with him. He is a great kheleke. We want him to join our outfit. He will be better off here with us than with those wimpy flowers. Talk to him about it. Convince him.

I am from Likhoele too, like him, added another Letlama man. Men from the same village must stay together. I bet our fathers looked after cattle together. They may even have gone to the same mophato. Children of a man should stay together.

Another man added, yes, we are children of a man. He is looking for his father. We can even help him there. I am sure Soalakahla can instruct the miners to look for that container as they dig for their gold.

More drinks were brought in. Not the home-brewed sorghum, hops or pineapple beer, but brandy and whisky. These men were loaded.

Women came in too. How could I not be joyful in the company of women?

Soon an accordion appeared on the instruction of the fat man, and the room, though tiny and crowded, turned into a famo party. I played Famole and I played myself. I even played 'U Ka Se Nqete', and both men and women went crazy. Everybody sang along for they knew every word of the hymn.

Cellphones were drawn and selfies were taken. Women swooned and said they never dreamed in their lives that one day they would see the hitmaker of 'U Ka Se Nqete' in the flesh.

Tau ea Khale kept on reminding me, don't you have a concert to play at?

8

Dirty-talking women

There is nothing as irresistible as a dirty-talking woman. The voice was hoarse as if she had been singing for the whole night. Maybe for many nights. It added to the allure. It was smoky. It was rough. Yet it was soft. Soft and smooth. And then gruff and angry again. Like clay ground mapped with cracks from a merciless sun. In times of severe drought. And then the rains. A voice that had seen many rains. Many droughts and many storms. Dry winters cold to the bone. And then the rains once more. It was stormy. It was breathless.

Seoeleoelele! Ao ... oeleoelele! Stop me before I spill out everything. Pele ke nya matsete. Before I shit out what has been hidden underground. Stop me before I tear your livers with secrets of how beautiful it is to love a woman. And to be loved by one. How to eat and be eaten until only crumbs of you are left on the plate.

I did not know what she was talking about. When a kheleke is good, it does not matter if you understand the meaning of the words. It is enough that they sweep you off your feet. They lift your spirit until it floats in the clouds. The rhythm and the cadence. And of course, the accordion. Though in this case I felt it was not doing justice to the woman's eloquence. Not that it was bad. To any ear it would be excellent. But it is my ear we are talking about.

Seoeleoelele! When she met me, I was an innocent child of the village. A faultless child who thought one day she would meet a man who would take out cattle for her and set her up in a homestead on the hillside. Yet I never even tried to look for such a man but ran away from those who approached me. Until deaths of strangers brought her to my father's compound.

Seoeleoelele! Jo nna 'm'e oeeeee! She made me discover the sacred bean. I always knew of its existence, of course. I felt its presence. But I did not know what it was there for, what it was doing hiding in the passage of life. Until she came and tickled it, and played with it, making me sing hallelujahs as a result. Jo nna 'm'e oeeeee!

Oh, beautiful blanket-wearers, the sacred bean! The one that ama-Zulu, People of the Heavens, of the Sky, offspring of Shaka, the one that they call msunu. Ao ... oe ... 'm'e oeee! People of Gauteng! People of the City of Lights, why do you call a terrible person, a despicable one, a reprobate without a shred of dignity, why do you call him msunu? Why turn such a beautiful part of a woman's body into an insult? How can such a pleasurable part of a woman be compared to the most awful person? How can such a glorious thing that never did anything to anyone, but is sleeping peacefully in its place of warmth, how can it be used to refer to those humans who are the scum of the earth and are devoid of humanity? Jo nna 'm'e oeeeee!

Seoeleoelele! Every time I see you, sister of a person, I die many deaths. Diva drive the car; the night is still young. Diva khanna koloi. Diva drive the car; my child is crying. Make love to me while the crickets are singing outside. While the frogs are croaking in unison in the ponds. Diva drive the car, step on the accelerator. Make love to me, you whores. Matekatse ting. Make love to me, you vagabonds. Diva step on the fat; make the petrol burn. Make love to me, bitches. Jo nna 'm'e oeeeee!

I had to see her with my own eyes. This voice that left you with desire for the owner, I had to see its owner. I just had to wake up despite the tired body that had spent the whole of the previous day exploring one shaft after another with the nameless one. This body that was not prepared to give up the search.

It was the second time we were doing this. The search for bones, I mean. The first was about two weeks before when I even missed a concert but ended up playing for some Letlama men. I had to come back again. And though we failed again yesterday, I would return. I was not prepared to give up finding my father though it had caused so much friction between me and my colleagues of the Cult of the Arum-Lily, and between me and Maleshoane, who suspected I was seeing some other woman. Otherwise why didn't I want to take her with me to this Durban Deep that had become an obsession?

The search yesterday was gruelling, and I was exhausted. Soalakahla arranged for a makeshift room inside Bob's Supermarket for me and the nameless one. The next day we planned to go down the shaft again.

It was important for me to rest. But the woman's voice did not allow that. Her hymns were provocative and filled me with desire for her, though I did not even know who she was or what she looked like. The looks would not have mattered anyway. Even if she were an eighty-year-old woman, with a face and limbs like sehoapa, with a voice like that, with hymns like those, she would have filled any man with desire.

I looked at the nameless one on a mat next to mine. He was fast asleep. What a boor! What man can sleep when such searing sounds are leaking though every crack of our shelter demanding attention? I groped for matches and lit the candle. The only thing I had to put on were my boots since I had slept with my clothes on. I sneaked out so as not to waken him.

It was in the early hours of the morning, perhaps around 3 a.m. or so, yet crowds were gathered outside a shack adjacent to Bob's Supermarket. That was where the hymns were coming from. I gradually pushed through the crowd, working my way to the door. A glimpse of her would be enough.

Seoeleoelele oelele oeeeeeeeeeee! Not only did this sister of a person help me discover the sacred bean, she made me discover the hymns. Not that I didn't know anything about them. I grew up surrounded by hymns. Hymns of the ramblers and wanderers. Hymns of the itinerants who spread love and joy in the countryside. Am I not the famed sister of a kheleke? Did my name not jump about in a kheleke's hymns?

After pushing and being insulted by those who felt I was bullying my way into the packed room, and after some of the folks recognised me as the hitmaker of 'U Ka Seng Nqete' and gave way and whispered the news to those in front, I finally reached the door and had a clear view of the singer. Sudden guilt hit me. Guilt? Shame! Sudden shame. I had desired my own sister, child of my mother. The figure of Noria standing tall in the crowd near the performer assured me that the singer was not someone who looked like my sister. It was Moliehi.

Seoeleoelele oelele oeeeeeeeeeee! Didn't a kheleke sing of my name? This sister of a person, she who wandered the countryside with a man who stole the grief of others, this sister of a person, she who opened my eyes that all this time I was yearning for a woman without knowing it, this sister of a person taught me how beautiful I am. How alluring. How seductive my voice was, and that it would be even more seductive if I sang hymns of love. Look at me now, whores and vagabonds. See how desirable I am. But your hanging things will yearn in vain without ever touching my sacred bean. It is only for the woman. Ao-oeeeee.

Women ululated and men cheered as she performed a final focho dance, and then disappeared into another room.

What a waste! What a waste of a good thing! joked the MC and the men in the audience agreed with him. They thought she too was joking. She was just being naughty. Just teasing them that she would rather give it to a woman than to them.

People were flowing out as I tried to push my way into the room. I managed to get to the MC guy.

I want to see the woman who was singing hymns here, I said.

Sorry, said the MC, she does not talk with followers, especially men.

In this business when they talked of followers, they meant fans.

I am not a follower, I said. I am her brother.

The MC laughed and said, Of course you are.

Really, I said quite earnestly, don't you recognise me?

As if I would know her brother, he said, walking away without taking a close look at me.

What kind of morons were these who did not recognise the hit-maker of 'U Ka Se Nqete'? Okay, most people listen on the radio. But I did appear on Bhodloza's programme on television as well. It occurred to me that it was easy not to recognise a star when you met him at a dump like this. You didn't expect him to be there. I followed the MC to the room into which my sister disappeared. He turned around and yelled at me.

170

What do you want now?

I want to see the singer, Moliehi, child of my mother, I said.

They have left, man, they are gone! yelled the MC.

Where to?

Do you think I know? They came here to play, and they left. How would I know where itinerant singers of hymns go when they are done? Did she arouse you that much?

You are talking shit, you mother's buttocks! I yelled back. She is my sister.

Shame returned. The ungodly feelings her voice wrought in my loins. The thoughts were incestuous whether I knew it was her or not. They were about the unknown singer. And the unknown singer was my sister.

You insult me by my mother again, said the MC glaring at me, my koto will taste the blood of your head.

I glared back at him unflinchingly.

Shame continued to eat me. I needed cleansing.

I couldn't sleep after that.

*

Maleshoane was cooking porridge for breakfast when I entered the kitchen. She was still in her nightdress with a tartan shawl around her waist. I thought she would be furious, but she was calm. I suspected it was the calm before the storm.

I sleep with my knees these days, she said.

Only last night, Shoane. You speak as if it is something that I do every day, I said.

I tried to kiss her, but she turned her head away. Not angrily. Gently.

Who is she? she asked. Who is the new woman you even miss concerts for?

Durban Deep, I said. That is her name. And I missed only one concert, two weeks ago.

Durban Deep. Still searching for your father's bones? I knew it. That's why you don't see me mad even though I know men are dogs. I knew it was about bones. Those bones will destroy your music just when it is taking off countrywide.

I ignored that. I had heard it before. She was becoming a nag about it. The bones were distracting me from the core mission – that of greatness. The other day she pooh-poohed the whole notion of appeasing the ancestors. Appeasing them for what? Why didn't they mind their own business while we carry on with ours here on earth trying to be great?

Do you think your father cares about a bunch of old bones lying in some mineshaft when he is busy having a great time with the rest of your ancestors? she asked.

I did not answer that question because I did not know things that happened in the land of those who are under the ground. My thoughts were on Moliehi.

Moliehi is somewhere here singing dirty songs, I said.

Somewhere where? She stopped ladling the porridge into a bowl and looked at me.

Somewhere in Gauteng, I said. I saw her, but she disappeared before I could speak to her.

Wait, she said. Let me go and serve Tau ea Khale his morning porridge so that you can tell me what you are talking about.

She was back in no time, demanding to know where I saw Moliehi. I told her about the famo party at some skanky place at Durban Deep. Of course, I am not a fool. I did not start the story from the beginning; the time when I had to wake up because some woman's

172

song had filled me with wanton thoughts, only to discover she was my sister.

*

Tau ea Khale was cooking us with lies about his days with MaRussia gangs. The less gullible among us knew they were lies, but we went along with his stories, nodding now and then, and exclaiming with wonderment. We were sitting on benches and beer crates in his backyard between his red-brick house and the corrugated-iron shacks that he had rented out to two tenants. All of us – the boy referred to as Tau ea Khale's eyes, Maleshoane, the children of the tenants and me – listened attentively and laughed raucously when the story called for it. One of the kids occasionally stoked the fire in front of us and turned the maize on the cob that was roasting on the embers.

It was like that in our days as MaRussia, said Tau ea Khale, chewing roasted maize.

I whispered to Shoane: He should be shot for lying to kids like this.

The children of today are going straight to Diablo, calling your own father's friend a teller of truth that's not true, said Tau ea Khale.

That's the problem with blind people; their hearing becomes so heightened that you cannot whisper about them behind their backs however softly.

It was like that, my children, said Tau ea Khale, stressing each syllable as if challenging me to dare contradict him. I was not up to the challenge, so he proceeded.

After fighting our battles with Masolo, or Machakane, or bo-Azikhwelwa, we craved for something salty. Even when we were not fighting any battle but were drinking all night and had a hang-over, we wanted something salty. And because we were MaRussia, we just walked into a Boer's farm and selected the fattest sheep. There were farms those days here in Gauteng. All those townships like Protea North and Protea Glen, they were the farms of the Boers. There were no houses but farms. We just walked into those farms and grabbed a sheep in broad daylight. No Boer could shoot us. We had powerful medicine men.

The other day you said it was a goat, said Tau ea Khale's eyes.

We are Basotho, said Tau ea Khale, with contempt in his voice, we hate the smell of goat meat. We rear them for the mohair. Okay, when a goat dies, we eat it because the grave of a cow or goat or sheep is the mouth. We eat the goat because it happens to be there, dead, waiting to be eaten. But we are partial to sheep. We are sheep people. So, it was a sheep that we stole from the Boers. If you want to insist that it was a goat, I'd rather stop my story right now.

We all begged him not to stop the story and admonished the boy for introducing goats in a story that was not his to begin with.

Tau ea Khale picked a row of kernels from the maize cob and passed it to the next person.

We walked back with the sheep on our shoulders. No one would dare approach a gang of MaRussia armed with sticks and the koto knobkerrie and ask us stupid questions about a sheep. We got to this very house, and in this very backyard we made a big fire and cooked the sheep in a big three-legged pot. The cast-iron kind that we used during feasts to cook for the whole nation.

Hau, ntate-moholo, you did not slaughter it first? asked Maleshoane.

We are MaRussia, snapped Tau ea Khale. We don't slaughter. We hit the beast with a koto on the head and while it's busy fainting we put it in the pot like that, with hair and all. Remember, we are MaRussia. We have not come to play here.

MaLemokhe? She used to be the head of police in the district where the Accordion Triangle, the home of great likheleke and famo music gangs, is located, said Mohalalitoe, now sitting on the beer crate vacated by Tau ea Khale's eyes.

Mochini remained standing, swaying and tapping his foot impatiently.

At that time, I was still one of the leading lights of the Train, continued Mohalalitoe, and MaLemokhe was one of us in that she gave us protection from the law. She was there when politicians used the Cult of the Train to form their party, then in opposition, which later became part of a governing coalition. I cannot say she was the one who encouraged a breakaway from the Train, using Semanya-manyane who later became her driver, but it happened. Mochini and I had left the Train already at that time, so what I know about this I learned from my spies inside the Train. MaLemokhe became a minister in charge of the national police and took the man with her to be her driver.

Maleshoane giggled and said, That sounds very fishy.

For you it would be, I said, because you are already thinking of things of the bedroom.

There are children here, you offspring of Diablo, said Tau ea Khale, chewing loudly, and passing the corn to Mohalalitoe.

I do not know how fishy it is, said Mohalalitoe, also crunching on the roasted maize. Things like that are not my concern. What I heard was that Khosi Mosotho Chakela was furious at the betrayal. Now he believes that the breakaway group of MaLemokhe and her driver, Semanyamanyane, is more of an enemy than Letlama.

What I heard was that the cabinet minister, when she was still chief of police, tried to broker peace between the famo gangs, by which they were referring to Lekhotla la Terene and Letlama, said Mochini, not to be outdone in showing off his knowledge.

Yes, said Mohalalitoe. That was long ago, when we were still with the Train. She and a group of businessmen from the district did try to bring the gangs together, but even then everyone knew those so-called peace-brokers were Khosi Mosotho Chakela's allies. That's why the peace failed. Men of Letlama knew it was meant for their destruction.

You don't like politics and politicians, I can see that, said Maleshoane.

Who can like politicians? They are crooks. If you mix your hymn singing with politics you are finished, said Mohalalitoe. Semanya-manyane is finished. Chakela will be finished. Perhaps not now. But it will happen soon.

Semanyamanyane is a Mosotho and has the right to take part in the politics of his country, I said. What if it is his conviction to be with these government people and their political party?

Tau ea Khale cackled and said, There is no political conviction in these famo gangs. It's all about competition for mejo – resources. Their allegiance to certain politicians is for their stomach.

But they are musicians; they are making money, chipped in a tiny voice timidly, fearful of being accused of participating in old people's discussions.

Not everybody makes money in the business of music, said Mochini. Your fame does not last forever. New musicians come in and take over. Let's go. I need to be at our mine in Krugersdorp.

Mohalalitoe stood up and said we should go into the house, if Tau ea Khale didn't mind, to talk some business. Tau ea Khale said his home was our home. Maleshoane said she was coming too, but Mohalalitoe stopped her.

I get the idea sometimes that you think you are a partner in this business, said Mohalalitoe.

It always disturbed me when Mohalalitoe called us a business. I was a man of music. A singer of hymns. A wanderer and, yes, sometimes a vagabond. I was a creator of happiness. How could anyone see what I do as business? As if I was selling candles, paraffin and sugar?

Mohalalitoe and I walked into the sitting room while Mochini went to the car to, as he said, fetch something.

I want to show you how serious we are about the Cult of the Arum-Lily so that you can also take it seriously, said Mohalalitoe as we took our seats at the table. Ever since you missed that concert in Diep-kloof it is difficult to trust your commitment to Mohalalitoe.

Hau monna, I exclaimed, we talked about that and you said it is forgiven and forgotten.

Forgiven yes, but not forgotten. Forgotten? Are you serious? How do I forget the embarrassment we went through, people screaming for the kheleke and demanding their money back, lies we had to tell that on your way to the concert you had an accident? You must thank Maleshoane for saving the day with her half-baked hymn singing and dancing. You must thank me too, who had to play the accordion for four hours. You must also thank the Men of the Flower who filled the stage and sang makhele and mangae to the joy of all. Forgotten? We are watching you.

Mochini returned with two big plastic bags and placed them on the table. He unzipped one and took out a purple blanket. He spread it on the table.

See what I am talking about? said Mohalalitoe. My own design.

It had ornate black-and-white designs of the arum-lily.

Our own special blanket just arrived from a factory in Harrismith, said Mohalalitoe.

He looked at me and was taken aback that I didn't seem to be impressed.

Do you know what this means?

A blanket in our colours, that's what it means, I said. So?

What do you mean so? He was furious.

Every famo group has its own colours, I said, puzzled as to why he was getting so hot under the collar.

No group has its own specially designed blanket, explained Mochini, scorn displayed on his face. Other groups wear blankets that anyone can buy in the shops, blankets from Robertson such as lefitori and seana-marena, and from other shops such as letlama. They were not specially made for those groups. This was made for us. No one else has it.

You designed this? I didn't even know you could draw, I said.

Obviously I was missing the point because Mohalalitoe was becoming apoplectic.

Listen, I explained to the White man what picture should be on the blanket, so yes, I designed it. But that is not the point. We now have a blanket we can be proud of because no one else has it. Only the Men of the Flower will wear it.

Our followers too, added Mochini. Didn't you say so?

Yes, our followers will be able to buy it from us, said Mohalalitoe. So, anyone who wears a purple blanket with the picture of the arum-lily will either be a Man of the Flower or a follower of the movement.

He gave me one blanket and I demanded that Maleshoane should have one as well. He reluctantly gave me the second one and warned me that next time any of my people, as he called them, wanted a blanket I would have to buy it.

You see, Mohalalitoe is getting places even though you are playing all these tricks trying to pull away from us, said Mochini.

I am not trying to pull away, I said. I just made one mistake.

It's not just the mistake, said Mohalalitoe, it is your attitude. We have eyes. We can see. You are a law unto yourself, without any loyalty.

It is because he has not been to the mountain, said Mochini.

180

That is one of the reasons, said Mohalalitoe. The mountain teaches you loyalty to your group. It teaches you manliness too. I think when we get back to Lesotho, we must sacrifice you for six months. You must go to a mophato. Mohalalitoe has a major mophato that we control, and we have a group of boys who will be going in this winter. I want you to join them.

I burst out laughing, which seemed to confuse them. But Mohalalitoe was determined to be patient with me. He explained that why it was important for me to go to lebollo – initiation school – was that it has a koma that could not be spoken about, broken or betrayed. It would teach me loyalty.

But the most important thing now is that the Cult of the Arum-Lily is growing, as you can see. You are doing a great job in music. But we also need your presence in mining. People in the mines are used to being led by a kheleke himself. They know I am a kheleke myself, but I am not the one with a hit single. We need to see more of you. Especially now that we are moving into the Free State.

This shocked me. I didn't know we were moving into the Free State. I thought we would be satisfied with Krugersdorp and Randfontein. The Free State was a very dangerous territory as the Cult of the Train had a stranglehold on all the illegal mines there.

We are breaking the stranglehold of the Train in the Free State, said Mohalalitoe, beaming. The leaders of the Train have involved themselves too much in the politics of Lesotho. They have been weakened as a result. When you allow yourself to be used by politicians, while you foolishly think you are using them, the music suffers, mining suffers, initiation schools suffer. Politics will be the end of the Cult of the Train.

You see why you must be hands-on in running the mines as well? asked Mochini. And to be respected by Basotho men you need to know koma, you need to graduate from initiation school, you need to be circumcised, you need to be a man.

Mohalalitoe said you are the one who is in charge of mining operations, I said. I think you guys should just leave me to the music.

I am in charge of the mining operations, but I cannot do it alone when the mines are many.

You see the lack of loyalty that I am talking about? said Mohalalitoe. You must go to the mountain. We'll take you there ourselves. You will be looked after very well by our special surgeons and teachers. You must be circumcised.

*

The three of us caught a taxi at Bree Street in the central business district of Johannesburg. Toloki, Maleshoane and me. Tau ea Khale wanted to come along too, but we said no. He tried to guilt-trip us by accusing us of discriminating against him because of his blindness. Instead of denying it, I agreed it was so because his blindness would be a handicap since we did not know where we were going. We did not know what problems we would encounter and wanted him to stay safe. We left him sulking, promising we would bring him nice things.

That was insensitive, said Maleshoane as we got into the taxi.

Would you rather he lied to the old man? asked Toloki.

He had arrived the night before, after I had given him the address in response to his text messages. He had left Lesotho and was on his way to England as the first leg in his search for mourning. But first he wanted to thank me for accommodating him and Noria, though that resulted in his brokenness. He also wanted to thank me for the money I left for him in payment for the accordion. It would come in very handy on his journey to the land of the White man across the seas.

He had been in Lesotho all along, staying at my father's homestead, which he said was crumbling ever since Moliehi and Noria deserted it.

At Likhoele his mourning practice had flourished, for people got to know him. He mourned at least two funerals a week, which was good enough to satisfy his yearnings. The rewards were small though, as the poor could not afford to pay a professional mourner, especially when mourning was something they could do themselves, albeit with less professional aplomb. Yet they still wanted to see him sitting on a mound mourning his heart out because that carried with it some prestige. After all, he was the man who was in the middle of things when men in purple blankets came and riddled a corpse with bullets. He was the man who was saved by the grave. And that was an important funeral with government officials, including cabinet ministers and military generals. To have such a man at your funeral, though you were a poor family, gave neighbours something to talk about.

Another reason the rewards were paltry was that most funerals were financed through life-insurance companies, and they did not cover professional mourning expenses. Some burial societies did pay him something since they were run by the community members themselves and could not say no when the bereaved family itself wanted to have a professional mourner grace their funeral.

By the time Moliehi and Noria abandoned the homestead he had learned to live with the fact that his relationship with Noria had ended and could not be repaired. He wouldn't have wanted to repair it anyway. After all, he had his pride as a man. Though Noria had been his childhood fancy, the dream that could not be fulfilled because his father had monopolised the stuck-up bitch, as his mother referred to her, until they met as adult homeboy and homegirl at some coastal city, and became lovers, and though there was such a long history between them, he was done with crying for her. She had chosen her new path; he would continue on his. He would cross the oceans, keeping to the original plan, and explore the world out there learning new of ways of mourning.

When did Moliehi become a singer of hymns? I asked.

Oh, at about that time, said Toloki. A year or so ago. She was encouraged by Noria, from what I could observe. They started attending famo parties in Likhoele. And there, I was told by her, she started freestyling with local accordion players. Then they started going far afield; to Matelile, to Thabana Morena, to small villages within the Accordion Triangle. They started spending days on end without coming home. In the meantime, your father's homestead was crumbling.

She used to hate all those things, I said. That child of my mother hated it when this boy-child played at famo parties.

I stayed in the mokhoro that you lent me, said Toloki, and I saw the food dwindling. No, they were not eating all those bags of maize and beans. They were selling most of that food. Bit by bit. They were selling the food and using the money to travel to one timiti after another.

Noria turned my sister into a vagabond! I screamed.

Noria turned your sister into a singer of hymns; into an itinerant musician; into an artist, said Toloki. The same thing she did to my father. Through her power a village blacksmith became an inspired sculptor of figurines. She herself cannot create. But she inspires people to create. I am glad I broke away from her creative spell.

You did not break away, said Maleshoane. She dumped you for a woman.

184

This was the same Maleshoane who called me insensitive when I said – no, merely implied – that Tau ea Khale would be a burden in our search for Moliehi.

The search itself was organised by Maleshoane when I was at a loss about where to go. First, I took her and Tau ea Khale to Durban Deep to the shack that held the famo party. It turned out it was run by one of Soalakahla's concubines who was happy to be of assistance to the famous kheleke who was always searching for the bones of his father at their mine. When Maleshoane told her we were looking for the woman who sang there the other night, she said, Oh, you want to recruit her to join your band? She must pay me commission for giving her exposure here at my humble establishment.

She told us they invited her from Vreugdeplek, another of those mines abandoned by the mining companies and now taken over by illicit miners.

I had heard of Vreugdeplek some time back when Mohalalitoe was thinking of invading it with his gang. I don't know what happened to that plan as I never really followed their mining adventures. I recall that the place was run by a gang from Mozambique, who were not even musicians but authentic miners who had been retrenched at formal mines. Later they were reinforced by amaXhosa miners who had been displaced by gangs elsewhere. Rival famo gangs were trying to take over Vreugdeplek, and pitched battles were fought. Mohalalitoe was trying to worm its way in by winning over the Mozambicans while the rest of the gangs were killing one another. He bought them generators which they would use underground to drill the rock in order to insert dynamite, and to provide some light as long as they were not used continually in closed spaces to accumulate deadly gas. Mohalalitoe was merely lulling the Mozambicans and their amaXhosa allies to sleep. By the time they woke up the whole mine and the squatter settlement around it would be under the control of the Cult of the Arum-Lily. That was the plan. But the Mozambicans were too smart to give in, hence Mohalalitoe's plan to invade them and mow them down with machine guns.

Maleshoane, Toloki and I were on our way to Vreugdeplek – Afrikaans for a place of happiness.

All the mines abandoned by mining companies that I had seen were nothing but devastation, including Durban Deep and our mines in Krugersdorp and Randfontein. I surprised myself by thinking of them in terms of *our* mines – including myself in the ownership. But, yes, I was of the Cult of the Arum-Lily and they were under the control of the Cult of the Arum-Lily. Blood was shed to acquire them; people died. I myself was not there. I was playing music. But by virtue of being a kheleke of the Cult of the Arum-Lily, they were mine. Blood and all. Devastation and all.

Vreugdeplek was even more devastated. When mining companies decided that the operations were no longer profitable, they did not rehabilitate the land after filing for liquidation. They just abandoned everything and took to other profitable ventures elsewhere, again scarring the land when the government was asleep, allowing the devastation to continue.

We walked among open sewers and gaping pits that no one had bothered to backfill. There were no warning signs, which made me wonder how many poor children had drowned in the toxic water in those ditches.

Vreugdeplek. Place of joy. I didn't see how there could be joy there.

After a few enquiries and missed directions we found a small shack built of cardboard, plastic sheets, old Masonite boards. It was the home of Noria and Moliehi. But no one was home. We stood outside for a while, not knowing what to do next. A drunken man with a phuza face came by, singing his drunken song. He passed us out-side the shack without seeming to notice us. And then he stopped as if hit by a sudden realisation that he had just walked past people.

You're looking for the s'tabane women? he asked.

All three of us stood there staring at him. I was offended that he was calling my sister a derogatory name that was usually used to refer to homosexual males. Since no answer was forthcoming from us, the man decided to move on. Then he stopped and shouted, ask the police. They know where they are. People tried to kill the singing one, right there near the door. The police took them. You can thank Bra Tools later.

Which way is the police station? asked Maleshoane.

Oh, so now you want to talk to Bra Tools when you were making yourself better? said the drunken man. Voetsek!

He staggered away.

Only then did I realise that the brown spots on the ground and at the makeshift door were splatters of blood.

If Mohalalitoe was paying you what is due to you, said Maleshoane, you would be having a car now. We would just be driving to the police station instead of walking, trying to find a taxi. You are a star, man. You shouldn't be walking like this while he drives a Mercedes-Benz.

We ultimately found the police station. Moliehi was on a stretcher on the veranda. Though her eyes were wide open she didn't seem to be conscious. Noria was standing next to her, holding her hand. Noria didn't betray any emotion when she saw us. No greetings were exchanged. All our eyes were on the woman lying on the stretcher.

She is the one whose beauty I sang about. Moliehi, child of my mother. And now she was lying there with a gaping wound on her head.

We are waiting for the ambulance, said Noria. She was still conscious when the police brought us here to make statements. And then, and then, all of a sudden ... maybe she lost too much blood.

An officer came out to find out who we were.

They almost killed her, he said, after the introductions.

Who are *they*? I asked.

We don't know, said the officer. I am told she is a famo singer. I would say it is part of the war of the musicians, but she is small fry. She wouldn't live in a shack like that if she were not small fry. Who would want to attack a small-time singer like that?

And then the police officer recognised me.

I have seen you on television. You are the guy who sings that popular song that is very silly.

You don't like it? I asked.

Oh, I like it, said the officer. Everyone likes it. Even people who don't care for famo music. If you say she is your sister, perhaps it has something to do with you. Are they not trying to get at you? Our detective might need a statement from you. Perhaps you will give them some leads.

The ambulance arrived and loaded her in the back. There was only room for Noria. Once more we had to find our way to the hospital. Once more Maleshoane made her snide remark about not having a car. This time there were some metered taxis around.

Noria was in the waiting room.

The doctor says she will be fine, she said. And for the first time looked at Toloki. There was sadness in her eyes. I did not know whether it was for Toloki or for Moliehi.

How are you? she asked. We have not seen you for a long time.

You have not seen me because you left me high and dry at Likhoele, said Toloki.

188

I hope you are not going to have a stupid lovers' quarrel now, I said, irritated. I want to know what happened to my sister.

We came back home from a timiti this morning, maybe four-thirty, and soon after our accordionist dropped us two men attacked us, said Noria. Actually, they didn't attack me, they attacked Moliehi. Even when I tried to get in between them and her, they merely pushed me aside and beat her up, one with a stick and the other with a machete.

Do you know these men? I asked. Who are they?

I don't know, she said. It could be anybody. Maybe some man we ignored or whose proposal we refused to entertain. Many men desire Moliehi, and when she says no they feel wounded. As you all know, men are dogs and think their penises are entitled to any woman they fancy.

There must be something more than that, said Toloki.

You don't know men, uena Toloki, said Maleshoane. They are like that.

Something more like what, Toloki? I asked.

Maybe the politics of your music, said Toloki. Just as the policeman suggested at the police station. People of your kind of music are always trying to kill each other. Remember, I was almost shot dead in a grave once. Almost killed by musicians.

I will get my Men of the Flower on to this, I said. Mohalalitoe will deal with them. No one attempts to kill my sister and gets away with it.

I was amazed at myself. I was embracing the gangster elements of Mohalalitoe – the Cult of the Arum-Lily. I was the kheleke, after all. They must come to my defence when my family was being violated. For the first time I felt like a gang boss. I must not be shy of being a gang boss. I must take the lead and fuck shit up.

Toloki asked us to leave for a while. He wanted to say goodbye to Noria since he had no intention of seeing her again.

As we waited outside Maleshoane laughed at me. I was finally taking my rightful place in the gang as one of the key leaders. I despised the fighting aspects of a hymn singer's life, but now I had seen that one could not always escape it, especially when one's family was violated.

Toloki did not take that long. He came out and said Noria wanted to talk to me alone.

I did not know what she wanted to talk to me about, but I started by accusing her of bringing Moliehi, child of my mother, to Gauteng to live the life of a vagabond.

You think you are the only one who can come to Johannesburg to seek your fortune in music? she asked. So can she.

You have messed up my sister's life, I said. Look where you are staying with her. Yet she has a home. With real houses. She has fields. She has a life. She had a life before you came.

You're not the only one who is a person, boy-child, said Noria. Moliehi wants to be here. She wants to be a kheleke, as great as Puseletso Seema. Tell you what, Moliehi will be a greater kheleke than you. Is that what you are scared of?

I wanted to scream. But what can one do with a woman like that?

You are a very cruel person, I said. See what you did to Toloki?

Leave Toloki out of this, she said. You do not know anything about us. You know nothing about the road we have travelled. You cannot speak on his behalf. He knows how to speak for himself, and he did. We have parted in peace because I love your sister.

You don't love anybody but yourself, I said, almost in tears. You enticed me into your bedding on the moseme mat in the mokhoro when Toloki was away. And now you are doing dirty things with my

190

sister. Things she is not even afraid to sing about. It's me today, my sister the next day. You eat everything in front of you.

It was only to make Moliehi jealous, boy-child, said Noria with piercing deliberation. Get over yourself. She knows that and we laugh about it.

9

Traitors

They said the leader of the Cult of the Train was old and arthritic and could not dance any more. They lied. They said he wanted to regain his youth vicariously through a younger hymn singer. They lied. I once admired him. I once tried to join Lekhotla la Terene. I am glad that I did not. That I failed even to have an audience with him.

They said his empire was crumbling. They said leaders of the Train were on the run. A man who could not dance because his knees were inflamed could not run.

They lied.

The new hymn was ''Mampoli''. It was not a hymn of hymns like 'U Ka Se Nqete'. They said boy-child, he whose body shall be dinner for the vultures, brother of Moliehi, is now singing politics. Boy-child, the one whose hymns were about love and the desires of the flesh, he is now singing of power and its vagaries. Is he becoming a warrior of death like his famo brothers?

They asked, who can this 'Mampoli be that this hymn is about? It is a sad hymn. Not a joyful one like 'U Ka Se Nqete'. Not a bouncy one. The accordion sounds like a church organ. It sounds like the funeral of a dignitary in the Roman Catholic Church. The Cathedral by the Circle. A funeral of an eater of money.

Of course, lovers of boy-child's songs danced to it too. No hymn of the wanderers could not be for dancing. Even the saddest. The angriest. The most bitter. The most venomous. People will dance to it.

That was why there were ten Men of the Flower on the stage, all in purple blankets as designed by Mohalalitoe, the man, and all dancing vigorously, brandishing sticks or knobkerries. Two were armed with kwakwa pickaxes. They joined in the song whenever I got to the chorus parts. And danced on both sides of me when it was my solo hymn part. There were no women dancers this time, not even Maleshoane.

She was not pleased when I told her that song was not for her, she would have to join the audience. It was supposed to be one of those manly performances that were serious and belligerent, and not the playful ones that we sang together.

We were backstage when I said this, and she was sulking.

Mohalalitoe and Mochini have won you over? she said.

It's give-and-take, Shoane, I said. They are right. Sometimes we must be warlike. We are famo musicians, after all.

Yes, they won you over, she said, shaking her head pityingly.

That's the only way we'll gain respect even from the gangs that attacked my sister, I said pleadingly. If I want Mohalalitoe to help me avenge my sister, then I must please them sometimes. This song attacks the Men of the Train. I start harmlessly by pleading to the ancestors to guide me to my father. But the hymn changes and ridicules the Men of the Train and their impending demise. It is a dangerous song. Leave it to me with the Men of the Flower. I don't want even a waft of danger to float near you.

I did not give her the opportunity to argue further. I leapt onto the stage.

Aoeleleeee, boy-child, food for the vultures! Man-eaters can never finish a man. Even when vultures swoop on him, boy-child will never be finished. You, Father of Lights, the one who is called Ramaseli, light my way in the deep mineshaft of Durban Deep, mohohlong oa lihele, the gaping hole of hell, light my way so that I find my father's bones. Aoeleleeee Aoeleleeee!

Seoelele oelele!

That was Maleshoane's voice, loud and clear. A phefa voice. Clean, smooth and piercing the eardrums. It came from the backstage area. She was defying me. I had never rehearsed this song with her. But there she was, landing on the stage, her purple blanket on her left shoulder, brandishing a stick in her right hand like a man of war.

She jumped about in a ridiculous tlala dance in front of the Men of the Flower, waving a stick as if challenging them. She hit their sticks with hers, creating a violent rhythm. This was the kalla dance, a pretend stick fight. The Men of the Flower were enjoying this provocation by a woman; they had big smiles on their faces instead of the angry mien they were supposed to maintain when performing the playful clash of the sticks.

Seoeleleeee, they tell me this boy-child spends his life in the dark intestines of the earth looking for an old man who is peacefully resting with the ancestors. Boy-child, brother of Moliehi, they tell me your obsession with bones is killing the joy out of your hymns. Your father's bones are squeezing the breath out of your song. Aoeleleeee boy-child, come back to the world of the living. To the

194

world of men. Ao shame, boy-child is crying for daddy. Baby boy-child wants daddy. Jo nna oeeeee!

I thought she had gone too far. She was going beyond banter, and I didn't find it funny.

Seoeleoelele! They say baby boy-child has gone to the mineshaft in search of bones. I was not there, but those who were there say a nameless man took him to the iron container that buried his father. Deep across the underground rivers where only ghosts live. They say the nameless one took him to a skeleton that he claimed was boy-child's father. But boy-child shook his head and said, Haaik'hona banna this cannot be my father. My father was not this small; these are the bones of a child. The nameless one was unfazed. How can you be fazed by anything when you have been paid such a lot of money? He was unfazed and he said, it is the bones of your father when he was still a boy. Jo nna oeeeee, the nameless one has already eaten the money. Jo nna oeeeee!

The audience was dying with laughter in the aisles and on the seats. Especially when she danced her fat-woman's unfulfilled focho.

She was wide-eyed when I grabbed her and pulled her by the sleeve of her seshoeshoe blouse to the side, and out of the stage door. The Men of the Flower remained on the stage singing, brandishing their weapons, and generally having the time of their lives without a kheleke hogging all the limelight.

I don't like it, Maleshoane, I said urgently. I don't like it at all.

You don't like what? Me singing with you in your so-called man song?

You making fun of my father, I said.

I am not making fun of your father, but of your obsession with him. He is dead, monna.

He leads me still, I said. I wouldn't have found Moliehi if I had not gone to Durban Deep to look for him.

Who says Moliehi wanted to be found? Have you ever thought of that?

Don't follow me onto that stage again unless you really want to regret it for the rest of your life, I said. I am not playing, Maleshoane. I am not playing.

I played a few bars on the accordion to warn the makhele chorus men that my hymn was about to resume and did a long-legged tlala dance cutting through the men to the front. The accordion held high above my head as if it were as light as a concertina. I made it wail.

Aoeleleeee! I am boy-child, kabela manong! Aoeleleeee Aoeleleeee! Don't listen to women whose rude tongues try to lash this boy-child to humiliation. Aoeleleeee!

Aoeleleeee Aoeleleeee! Boy-child is a man with gravitas, not a woman's plaything. He refuses to be provoked by the pettiness of skirts going pheu! pheu! in front of him. Boy-child is talking of the demise of men. The demise of 'Mampoli! The demise of his gang of the Train! Jo nna oeeeee!

The audience laughed. I wondered why when my hymn was not supposed to be funny. I realised too late that I had punctuated my hymn with Jo nna oeeeee! which was really a woman's cry. It did not go well with my new macho image and the song that was about things of the state. I had to keep on reminding myself of the new warrior image I was trying to cultivate.

Aoeleleeee Aoeleleeee! 'Mampoli is in a qhafu-qhafu of shit and leaders of the Train are on the run. Don't ask me about it, I, boy-child, Man of the Flower, ask those who know. Those who were there. I can only tell you what they say. I can tell it all in glee and in satis-faction. They say it all started when leaders of the Train helped 'Mampoli to form his political party. And they sang hymns in his praise. And nations gathered to dance to their hymns. Nations fell in love with 'Mampoli as the anointed one. Nations followed him to the polls until he became the government of the day. Aoeleleeee!

Aoeleleeee Aoeleleeee! Men of the Train had their person as ruler of the land, the ruler of the land had a famo gang at his beck and call. Men of the Train own 'Mampoli, 'Mampoli owns Men of the Train. Who's owning who, who's fooling who?

Aoeleleeee Aoeleleeee! They say it is a story of wives and wives and wives. Of mistresses and concubines. Leaders of the Train are on the run. Don't ask me because I was not there. I can only tell you what they say. Don't make me a witness, I didn't see the deed with my own eyes. I only saw a police notice. They say they are looking for the leaders of the Train. Why are men of the law looking for Men of the Train, when the sun is so hot and the winters so cold? They say 'Mampoli's new lady, his seponono se likoti marameng, the beauty with dimples on the cheeks, wanted to be something called festiledi. They say this thing called festiledi is so important to have you can even kill for it. So, she asked the leaders of the Train to kill 'Mampoli's wife. You know the story, why do you want me to repeat it like someone whose finger has been tied with twine? You know how 'Mampoli's wife was riddled with bullets. You know how 'Mampoli's lady became festiledi and later married 'Mampoli. You know how you asked, Don't you marry first and then become festiledi?

Aoeleleeee Aoeleleeee! They say 'Mampoli lost his power, festiledi is in jail, and the leaders of the Train are on the run. Festiledi is out on bail. Festiledi is facing a murder trial. They say festiledi used to dance to the hymns of the Train. Big loudspeakers blaring. Festiledi cannot dance any more. 'Mampoli cannot dance any more either. He was never a dancing champion anyway.

Aoeleleeee Aoeleleeee! Welkom, we are coming. Welkom, we are taking over the mines. The Cult of the Arum-Lily will sweep away the rubbish and take over Welkom and the whole of the Free State. Prepare for the funeral. The Train is the deceased. Soon we'll be singing 'Haufi le Morena' for the Train. Nearer my God to Thee. Aoeleleeee!

Mochini went crazy with the drums. Mohalalitoe stood in the aisle cheering and dancing, his stick raised and his purple blanket flying in all directions as he spun like a top.

*

You sing about things you know nothing about. That is going to be dangerous for you. What if there is a trial and they are acquitted? All of them, including 'Mampoli who we hear has been charged as well. What will happen to your song? That was Maleshoane bombarding me with questions so early in the morning.

I was not in the mood for an argument. My head was pounding from last night's hangover. I didn't usually drink, you know? Even during those days of the concertina when I wandered the country-side playing the timiti circuit I hardly drank. Yes, occasionally I would have some pineapple, hops or sorghum beer, what my people called thabisa lihoho. But I was never the kind of drinker who went lights out. Until last night.

Mohalalitoe and Mochini took me to a braai in Phiri where a lot of Basotho were gathered buying plates of food with plenty of meat and drinking a lot of beer. I think it was a stokvel. They refused when Maleshoane wanted to come along and I didn't defend her this time. I was still annoyed with her for trying to humiliate me during my performance.

This is what I was talking about, boy-child, said Mohalalitoe. It is this kind of song that Mohalalitoe should be singing, threatening the enemy, taking the war to him.

He was elated, and a plate of curried tripe, dumpling and spinach in front of him made for a perfect night. In front of me too. And in front of Mochini, although his was with beanless samp. Though Mohalalitoe used a spoon to eat the food we would normally eat with our hands, grease still ran down his arm. More of it ran down his chin leaving spattered yellow spots on his shirt. Mochini was just as ecstatic, more so because he had outdone himself on the drums and on the chants, while the Men of the Flower delivered chants that touched even the hardest hearts of warriors. He deserved the quart of Black Label beer in front of him which he guzzled directly from the bottle.

We scared him when we threatened him with circumcision, said Mochini, laughing. Now he will toe the line.

It was not a threat, said Mohalalitoe. Circumcision is still necessary. Especially now that the Cult of the Train is in shit and we'll be capturing their territory. The Men of the Arum-Lily are all circumcised. They are not happy to be led by a man who does not know the secret of the mountain, though he may be a kheleke of the world.

I laughed, trying to force the conversation in a different direction.

So, now you admit I am a kheleke of the world? I said.

I have never not admitted that, said Mohalalitoe. Why do you think we approached you to join us? The only thing I hated about you was your stubbornness, your refusal to do away with useless woman songs and to sing warrior songs instead. Now that you have come with this one called ''Mampoli'', I am telling you, there will be peace in the world.

But you still have to go to the school of the mountain, said Mochini.

This annoyed me. Why was he bent on spoiling my evening?

And I suppose you will make me? I said standing up and glaring at him from above as he looked up at me from his chair. Why don't you do it now?

The woman of the house was quick to notice that someone was gearing for a fight. She came rushing to our table.

You don't come here to do stupid things at my stokvel, she said turning her angry gaze from me to Mochini and then to Mohalalitoe.

Don't worry, 'Mamosali, said Mohalalitoe. You know with young people, they are quick to flare up, but their balls are still not hard enough to stand a fight. You will not see a fight from anyone of us here. Plus, we are all Men of the Flower.

A drunken follower saw me and rushed to our table.

Jo! Banna! This is the brave kheleke who provokes the Cult of the Train directly. You are fearless. You even come to Phiri, which is their turf.

I didn't even know that Phiri was a territory under the sway of Banna ba Lekhotla la Terene. Mohalalitoe looked at me and smiled.

That's why we are here, he said. Immediately after provoking them with the song. Let's see what they can do about it.

When I looked around, I realised that most of the men at this stokvel were people I had performed on the stage with. Only about two of them were in purple blankets. The rest were not wearing blankets at all. The devil, Mohalalitoe, had brought us here to provoke a war. He looked a bit pissed off that no one was taking the challenge.

The follower was jumping up and down around us in fawning admiration.

They say Men of the Train are very angry, said the follower. They heard of your song. They say there is no DJ who will ever play it, they all fear for their lives. You see, you did something very unusual there, kheleke. You called them by name in your song.

200

I didn't call anyone's name, I said.

No, you gave them nicknames, said the follower. But you called the Cult of the Train by name. That's why they are angry. They say you sing shit about them.

That's what I like about that song, said Mohalalitoe. It calls them by name. Anyway, what can they do about it? They dug their own grave meddling in the politics of Lesotho and in the love affairs of politicians.

Indeed, what I did was unusual. It was not bravado but folly. Famo bands dissed each other all the time. But they never called each other by name. They used the kobisa language – referring to each other obliquely so that the listener reads between the lines or just suspects to whom the threats are directed. Sometimes they were not threats at all. Just scorn. Provocative words meant to demean. All in the kobisa language.

Mine were certainly threats of weeding them out of the mines and taking them over. Only through outright pitched battles could that be achieved. Mine were therefore threats of war. I was using direct language instead of kobisa because I knew they were at their weakest, with their leaders on the run. Who knows, they may be hiding in the very shafts we planned to invade.

Both Mohalalitoe and Mochini-oa-Ipommpa were so chuffed with my new outlook that they pumped me with all sorts of liquor, ranging from beer to Scotch, to brandy, to wine. They kept on reminding me that they had never socialised with me to this extent, so I must take advantage of it and make them happy.

What if the Men of the Train attack us when we are drunk? I asked. You said we are in their territory.

I hope they do, said Mohalalitoe. We are ready for them.

After that, lights out.

I only regained my senses when Mohalalitoe dropped me outside Tau ea Khale's gate in Senaoane in the morning hours. Mochini was giggling that I was so drunk I had a blackout in the middle of a conversation.

Voetsek, I said as I staggered out of the car.

Maleshoane had not slept. Apparently I had collapsed at the gate when she found me.

I don't know why I am still up at this time waiting for a shit like you, she said, as she dragged me into the house.

And then the upbraiding began. I was going to find myself in deep shit one day, taking the rivalry between the famo gangs to this extent and being in the pocket of Mohalalitoe and Mochini and failing to defend her when Mohalalitoe said she couldn't come along to the stokvel and refusing to sing with her, though 'U Ka Se Nqete' wouldn't have been a hit without her, and I was full of shit and would end up in a shit bucket.

All this time I was closely studying her mouth as she spoke. It was twisted as if she was in great pain. It looked so inviting; pain has its moments of beauty. I couldn't help but grab her and plant a kiss on it.

*

You see a beautiful thing; you want to share it with somebody. I had no one to share beautiful things with. Until Noria came along.

She was lying on the floor as she said this. Moliehi, child of my mother, was lying on the floor with only a threadbare donkey blanket between her battered body and the hard floor. Hard ground, in fact, rather than floor. Things should be called what they are.

There was not a single chair around. No table. Nothing that passed for furniture. We sat on the ground next to her sprawling body.

I understand what you are saying, said Maleshoane. I am in the same situation. It is the same reason I am still with your brother even though he is full of shit.

Noria is not full of shit, protested Moliehi.

That's not what I am saying, said Maleshoane.

You should come with us, child of my friend, said Tau ea Khale. We will nurse you back to health. I have a daughter-in-law and grandchildren who will look after you until you are strong enough to go your way. None of us can stop you being with your Noria, even though for us old people it is shameful, except when you are a diviner or traditional healer or the Rain Queen who can only marry other women. It is the thing of you young people. You love whoever you love. We'll not interfere with that.

And you are not the Rain Queen, I added. You are not a healer either. So, get over yourself and this Noria person.

I can be both if I want, said Moliehi.

No, you can't, said Tau ea Khale. You're just being stubborn now. Just like your father. He was hard-headed. There is only one Rain Queen and she and all her wives live with her Balobedu people in the Limpopo Province. As for being a healer, it's a calling. It's not something you do on a whim just because healers are permitted by the ancestors to have lovers and spouses of the same sex and you are desirous of another woman.

Noria is not a whim, old man, said Moliehi, groaning. I did not know whether it was in pain or because of the words of Tau ea Khale.

She tried to turn and face away from us. She groaned some more and stopped trying.

And where is this Noria of yours? I asked. How can she leave you alone like this when you are obviously in so much pain?

She's gone to do piece jobs for the miners so she can buy food for us, said Moliehi.

Listen to the word of a greybeard, child of my mother, I said. We just want you to get well.

I am well, she said. Well, almost.

She was not. Her head was still in fresh bandages. She only got there the day before. That's what the hospital told us. We first went there thinking that she might still be there judging from the kind of injuries we had seen on her. But they told us that she had been discharged to save the bed for other patients and would be treated as an outpatient. We were quite shocked when we got to the shack to find that she was still in a bad way. Hence our cajoling her to allow us to take her with us so that we could nurse her to better health. She, on the other hand, thought we just wanted to take her away from Noria.

She is stubborn like your father, said Tau ea Khale. Yet she looks very much like you. One could think that you are twins.

Are you just pretending to be blind? asked Maleshoane. How do you know what she looks like? Because indeed she does.

Her voice tells me, said Tau ea Khale.

In truth you are definitely blind, said Moliehi. She was getting a bit light-hearted now. She even giggled. And then groaned from the pain of giggling. Only a blind man can say I look like this ugly man.

You are treading on sacred ground now, Moliehi, said Maleshoane. Be careful not to insult me. Your brother may be full of shit, but he is not ugly. Do I look like someone who would go out with an ugly person?

I did hear that you are going around with a blind old man, said Moliehi, who has now proved he is really blind. What is this all about?

You daughter of Diablo. Be careful what you say about me.

204

He is my living ancestor. He knew our father, Moliehi. I feel my father's presence through him. His wisdom leads me to places where my father would have led me.

And all this time I thought you liked me for myself, said Tau ea Khale feigning a sulk.

Once more Moliehi giggled. She managed to do it without contorting her face in pain this time. I could see in the woman lying on the floor a fuzzy image of the Moliehi of Likhoele, skipping about joyfully. The Moliehi of my songs. The Moliehi of home, by the winter brazier. I was even more determined to take her away from there.

It is not from Noria that I want to take you, I said. You are an adult. Your love is your life. You love whom you love. You share beautiful things with whom you want to share beautiful things. It is from a dangerous situation that I want to take you.

I didn't want to tell them about my encounter with Soalakahla yesterday, but I just had to, if only to make Moliehi realise the danger she was in.

I had gone to Durban Deep alone, without the nameless one. There were two things I wanted to discuss with Soalakahla; firstly, I was tired of paying such a lot of money each time to be allowed down the shaft, and I suspected that he and the nameless one were on some scheme to drain more cash from me while taking me on a bootless errand. This thought was put in my head by Tau ea Khale some days before, only as his suspicion, and it kept on eating me. I wanted Soalakahla to be aware that I was not a total moegoe who had come to be eaten here in Johannesburg. Secondly, the first time I saw Moliehi she was performing at his concubine's joint. I needed to find out how they knew Moliehi, how she got to be playing there, and most importantly if there were any conflicts of which they were aware that could lead me to her attackers. The attack was on her, not on Noria. There must be a reason.

Soalakahla was happy to see me. He said he had been expecting me.

You come to our mine a lot and we welcome you like the gentlemen we are even though you belong to a rival gang, he said. I've been given the mandate to invite you to join Letlama. It is not the first time we do so.

You know I am a Man of the Flower, I said, laughing.

I thought he was joking. They all knew I belonged to a different famo group. Even that first night when I played for the leaders of Letlama they all knew that I was from Mohalalitoe. They even joked about it, and suggested playfully that from then on they counted me as a Letlama ally.

But you keep on coming to our mine, said Soalakahla. I think you are really yearning to be one of us.

Tell your bosses I am happy where I am.

From what I hear you are not happy at all, said Soalakahla. They treat you like a servant instead of the kheleke you truly are. What kheleke do you know who is not the leader of his gang?

As if I'd be a leader if I joined Letlama. You have likheleke of your own who lead Letlama. You have deadly men like Lekase. What makes you think a kheleke of my standing would have a place in Letlama?

Of your standing? he asked mockingly. You are good but you are not of the stature of Lekase. Or of Mahlanya. But still you would have a respected place in Letlama. You are out of place with the upstarts of the Flower.

The banter was still friendly at this point. But soon he became menacing. He told me that this would be the last time I put my foot on the hallowed grounds of Durban Deep. Of Vreugdeplek as well; he knew my sister lived there. They were in the process of taking it over from the Mozambican and amaXhosa gangs – whom he called Machakane le Maqhotsa.

You are either with us or with the enemy, said Soalakahla. We won't allow you here if you are not with us. If you are not with us and we see you here, we'll kill you. And by the way, as a pasela, we'll kill your sister too.

So, it's Men of Letlama who attacked her? I suspected this. You bastards!

I wouldn't be in a rush to throw around insults if I were you, said Soalakahla with a sneer on his lips. How do you know it's Letlama? I am not saying it's not. And I am not saying we won't kill her completely if you keep on playing games with us, refusing to be our leader.

Then he broke out laughing. He thought he had said something brilliant, killing me and my sister for refusing to join his famo gang and taking up a leadership position by virtue of my eloquence.

And by the way, he added, I do not know anything about this. That is why I cannot say it was Letlama. I was not there. I run the mine. The only thing I know about is gold. Oh, another thing I know besides gold is that there is talk around that your sister was attacked by Mohalalitoe. Yes, the very Mohalalitoe after whom the Cult of the Arum-Lily was named. He is not happy with you. He could easily attack your sister to make you toe the line. He heard of your shenanigans, visiting and even sleeping in Letlama territory. He wants to bring you back to your senses. He could even kill your sister if you continue your wayward ways.

I was dealing with mad people here. I walked away. I kept on looking back in case he was aiming a handgun at me. Or even a rifle. Those blankets were hiding places for rifles. Letlama people were famous for being the most brutal killers in the business. They became like that because of the Cult of the Train. In the early years Letlama people were badly treated by Lekhotla la Terene who were armed by the police. That made them bitter and vicious and killing machines who were not scared to have a shootout with the police at a police station. I kept on looking back. But Soalakahla was just standing there, one arm akimbo, the other hand waving at me like he was Queen Elizabeth herself. When I was some distance away, he called me in the friendliest of tones.

Hey, boy-child, take your pick.

I had to tell this whole story to show Moliehi that her life was in danger.

If I die, I die, said Moliehi. Whoever kills me between these friends of yours, my blood will be on your conscience. That's why you are so eager to save me, it is from things you yourself have caused.

You keep big things like these from me? said Maleshoane.

You didn't even tell me anything like this, said Tau ea Khale. You went to Durban Deep alone. How can I be your living ancestor if you keep such secrets from me?

*

It was the hottest concert yet, at least since the days when 'U Ka Se Nqete' was new and causing all the excitement. The church hall in Mapetla was packed, and the wooden floors were booming with stamping feet. A fight did break out among some members of the audience, but the Men of the Flower soon quelled it.

I performed the warrior song, ''Mampoli', and the love song, 'U Ka Se Nqete'. In both hymns Maleshoane featured and did her thing. In ''Mampoli' she herself was a true fighter and danced the dance of warriors, not the one that teased men to a point of desire. She challenged men to war instead, clashing her stick with theirs in a furious dance. Mochini-oa-Ipommpa was a star. Not the star of the show. That could only be me. And maybe Maleshoane. But he was a star in his own right. People underestimate how much a drum enhances the rhythm of famo music. It can only be to the rhythm of the drum that women move their bums in the sexually suggestive fecha dance movements.

After the show Maleshoane was cheerful. She was praising me all the way to Senaoane, which was the next township anyway and was not too far away. Mohalalitoe was driving and Mochini was sitting next to him in the front seat. They were just as excited. Maleshoane had not been a bad idea after all. She reminded the audience a lot of Puseletso Seema who was reputed to be a woman of the gun. Maleshoane herself could be a woman of the gun too. She was as good as any man.

If you had asked me, I would have told you I am better than any man, said Maleshoane.

The two men laughed. I didn't. It was not a joke.

Tau ea Khale woke up when he heard our voices and joined us in the sitting room.

Now we have woken up the old man, said Maleshoane. Sorry about that, ntate-moholo.

Mohalalitoe placed a case of beer on the table.

Don't be silly, do you think I will be left behind when there is beer? asked Tau ea Khale. I could smell it from the cans even before they are opened.

We must celebrate, said Mohalalitoe. You have outdone yourself. You outdo yourself like hell these days. That new song, where you kobisa the enemy! That song is fire!

It is not even kobisa, said Mochini opening a can of beer. It is telling them directly. It is calling out the Cult of the Train by name. You saw their supporters trying to start a fight during the concert?

Did they tell you you have visitors, son of my friend? asked Tau ea Khale. They have been accommodated in the backrooms by my renters.

Maleshoane said she suspected who they were. She rushed out of the kitchen door, and in no time returned with Moliehi and Noria. Mochini spotted them first as they entered from the kitchen and said, Oh, your sister has healed now, has she?

Child of my mother, you came! I cried.

How do your friends know that Moliehi has healed? asked Noria. Healed from what?

Nobody tried to answer Noria. I was asking myself the same question. I remembered Soalakahla.

We have come to talk to you, said Moliehi, looking at me.

Although there was a lot of space available, the two women didn't seem to be interested in taking seats. Maleshoane took a seat and gestured at the sofa to the ladies. They didn't budge but stood next to my chair.

I just want what is best for you, child of my mother, I said.

We cannot talk here among these people, said Noria. We just want you to stop bothering Moliehi, to let her live her life. But we'd rather talk in private.

My children, you have the whole day tomorrow to talk about these things, said Tau ea Khale. We keep private matters private in this house.

The beautiful one is right, said Mohalalitoe. Your family matters are your business. We are here to celebrate. Join us. This is no time for war. You know what we are celebrating?

He was passing cans of beer around.

The successful concert, I said. The hymns. ''Mampoli'!

Even more than that, said Mohalalitoe. Things are shaping up well all round. We are about to take over Vreugdeplek.

Is that not where you ladies come from? asked Mochini.

How do you know that? asked Noria.

Those Mozambican and Maqhotsa gangs in Vreugdeplek were operating under the government of the Cult of the Train. Not many people knew that. But now that government is in disarray because the leaders of the Train are on the run. Men of Letlama thought they would grab it for themselves. By force. We have fought pitched battles with them because we also want that mine. But then, because we are smart, we bought the miners generators to light inside the shafts and also to power-drill holes where they insert dynamite to break down the rock walls. Now those Mozambicans are fighting on our side against the Men of Letlama.

The greatness of the Flower, declared Mochini.

But they say boy-child is a man of Letlama, said Noria.

We all laughed. But Noria was serious.

Soalakahla told me he goes to Durban Deep all the time, said Noria. He spends a lot of time with the Men of Letlama.

Where do you come across Soalakahla who tells you all these lies? I asked.

One of his women gives Moliehi a gig sometimes. So, we go to the mines of Letlama a lot.

It is not a difficult thing to explain, said Tau ea Khale. I took him there the first time to look for his father.

So, this is true? Boy-child, you are betraying us? asked Mohalalitoe.

Tau ea Khale has told you why I go to that mine, I said.

I don't believe you, said Mohalalitoe.

I don't believe you either, said Mochini. You think we are children. You are a sell-out. Do you know what they did with sell-outs during the days of motsabalatso? They put tyres around their necks, poured petrol in them and set them alight. You are a traitor! That's always the problem when you deal with men who have not been to the school of the mountain.

I saw Noria flinching as Mochini described the treatment of sell-outs.

Men? Boys! said Mohalalitoe. He is a leqai, that is why he is betraying us. An uncircumcised boy. He does not know the secret koma, the song of the mountain.

He was standing up and was looking down at me on the chair. I stood up so as to face him eye to eye. He was frothing at the mouth.

I am tired of hearing that same song over and over again, I said. So, you can take your circumcision and eat it. You will not see me there.

Maleshoane broke out laughing. Everyone looked at her as if someone had accused her of releasing gas in good company.

Why, well, it is funny, she said. Don't you think? Eating circumcision?

All I am saying is if I am a traitor then you are a traitor too. You betrayed the Cult of the Train, stealing their secrets to form your own organisation. Koma didn't teach you anything because you continue to be a crook eating the money of the Cult of the Arum-Lily. Do you think I am blind to the fact that you have been robbing me and everyone else?

So, you are admitting that this woman is telling the truth?

This woman is lying, I said.

I am not lying! screamed Noria.

I mean the way you put it, I said. You are lying when you say I work with Letlama. I have been at the mine, yes, but I don't work with Letlama.

Noria took out a cellphone from her handbag and showed him a picture.

So, who is this, eating life with Letlama people? asked Noria. I got this from Soalakahla.

She shoved the phone at me. It was me all right in the picture. With a strange accordion. Jollifying with men in letlama blankets. That first night when I entertained them, missing my concert at Diepkloof Hall.

Mohalalitoe snatched the phone from my shaking fingers. He stared at the picture for a while. He too was shaking. And then he threw a swift right punch at me. I ducked. Noria caught the phone as it flew out of his hand. I teetered a bit and quickly recovered my balance but did not punch back. Instead I moved back a little from the range of his arms. Mochini tried to hold him back. He broke loose and came furiously at me. I gave him a good left punch that left him reeling. I could see hazily that he had drawn a gun. I could see hazily Noria diving between us. I could hear a shot ring as if from a distance. I could hear vaguely its reverberation. I could see Noria falling to the floor. Immediately followed by me. I could hear distant screams. Moliehi's. Maleshoane's. I placed my hand on my stomach. I could feel warm blood through my fingers. Sticky. It could only be blood. But there was no pain.

A frozen moment. Frozen screams. My eyes were wide open. Noria lumped on top of me. But there was no pain. Mohalalitoe and Mochini towering over us.

See what you have done! Mochini yelled at Mohalalitoe.

Sorry, said Mohalalitoe.

Let's go, said Mochini.

Mohalalitoe just stood there, stunned, gun in hand pointing at the floor. Pointing at his own feet. Mochini grabbed him by the arm and dragged him out.

But there was no pain.

10

The end is always a journey

There is a time for everything, said the preacherman. We didn't even know his name. We picked him at the bus stop in the marketplace in the camp of Mafeteng. He was preaching to the heathens who went about their business without paying attention to him. He cursed them for ignoring the Word and went on regardless. That was where Moliehi found him. For all we knew he could have been a charlatan. How do you tell? And who are we to judge? If he says he is a man of God, then he is a man of God.

Come and bury our person, she begged.

Go to your church, the preacherman said. I have never buried anyone. Me and the dead don't mix.

There's always the first time, Moliehi said.

I am just a street preacher. Never been ordained by anyone. Leave me out of it.

There was an honest street preacher for you. Moliehi said that's exactly who we wanted. And, of course, the promise of a few maloti made him change his mind fast about not mixing with the dead.

We had no church to go to. Our mother used to be a Santa woman of the Catholic Church. But after she passed on, we never bothered to continue her tradition. So, Ntate Fatere, the priest of the Ma-Roma, said he knew nothing about us. He would not bury our dead. We did not belong to him, nor to his Christ. Ministers are very strict nowadays. They don't bury people from families that never tithed in their church. Money talks. The way to heaven has expensive gatekeepers.

And a season for every activity under the heavens, continued the preacherman. He was reading from Ecclesiastes in his tattered Bible. A time to be born and a time to die.

At this point Toloki's controlled wails tapered off and were replaced by a crescendo of heartrending outbursts, Noria! Noria! Noria! Vuka, Noria! Vuka, sihambe! Vuka, sigoduke, Mama ka Vutha! Wake up, Noria! Wake up, let's leave. Wake up so we go home, Vutha's Mother.

He was sitting on the mound by the gaping grave, swaying from side to side. His face was drenched in tears. And in mucus that he kept rubbing off with the back of his hand. This was a new Toloki. The old Toloki never cried tears when he mourned the deaths of strangers. He performed mourning. He imbued it with graceful-ness. And pizzazz. This was not a stranger lying in the coffin. This was Noria. This was no performance. This was no professional mourning. This was mourning. Full stop.

Toloki's cries startled Moliehi out of her reverie. She let go of the handgrips of my wheelchair. It began to roll down the crag. Slowly. I had foolishly not employed the brakes. I was not used to this damn thing yet. And my arms were still weak. My whole upper half, in fact. While my lower part was dead. Paraplegia, they said at Barag-wanath. Though I was done with in-hospital treatment, I still needed months of rehabilitation.

The wheelchair had moved only a few inches when she grabbed it by the armrest and pushed it back. The drama did not draw the attention of the small crowd at the graveside. They were all focusing on the sight of this stocky grieving man, rendered even uglier by ungovernable body fluids. And at the ragtag preacherman who seemed stunned for a moment, but who soon remembered his task and went back to Ecclesiastes.

A time to plant and a time to uproot. A time to kill and a time to heal.

The time to heal was only for me, not for Noria. There was only time to kill when it came to her, though she was not the killer but the killed. Once you are dead you cannot heal. She took a bullet that was meant for me. She dived between me and Mohalalitoe's handgun. The 9 mm bullet penetrated her shoulder and passed out the other side into my body, and is now lodged in my spine. I spent a month as an inpatient, one surgery after another, while Noria spent a month in a mortuary. She had to wait for us. She had to wait until I was able to travel to Lesotho and until Toloki returned from foreign lands. She had to wait until Moliehi could make all the arrangements with the chiefs and overcome all the government red tape so that Noria could be buried in Likhoele, next to the grave of Moliehi's mother. Toloki was gracious enough to go along with that. Perhaps it was not a matter of graciousness. What choice did he have?

She is dead, Toloki had said. I cannot fight for a corpse. I can only mourn it. After all, she chose you when she was still alive. It is you who will bury her as you wish.

I paid all the expenses; the costliest was conveying her from Johannesburg to Lesotho.

216

A time to tear down and a time to build. A time to weep and a time to laugh. The preacherman had to yell those words so that we heard them clearly above Toloki's inconsolable screams beseeching Noria to wake up so that they could leave. Vuka, Noria, sihambe.

She didn't go with him when she was alive, Moliehi whispered to me. Why would she go with him now she's dead?

Don't be mean-spirited, I said.

She no longer seemed to be paying attention to the proceedings by the graveside. Her eyes were looking up the incline, to the fresh thatch of her house peeping above the escarpment.

She had worked on it relentlessly. I could only watch her from my wheelchair when she rebuilt our father's homestead. When we returned from Johannesburg all three houses were in ruins after months of neglect. She worked on each one to make them even better than they were before. She brewed sorghum beer so that those who came to help could have something to drink.

Our neighbours came. When there is beer people come. Quite often not for the beer itself but for the camaraderie. For the gossip. For the news of the fights and the killings of the famo gangs in the Land of Gold, and the deaths that spilled over to the villages of the Accordion Triangle, the origin of some of the most vicious musicians.

To the villagers we held a privileged position in telling the stories from the inside because I was reputed to be a kheleke of the Cult of the Arum-Lily, and by default a gang leader. Word had also gone around that I had been crippled for life in a gang war. My compatriots therefore looked at me in awe. But I could not entertain them with any gangland gossip. I just wanted to forget that I ever had any association with the pherese men, as the villagers referred to them. So, they gave up on me and focused on drinking the beer and helping Moliehi.

It was indeed time to build.

I wondered what Moliehi, child of my mother, was staring at. Then I saw the figure walking down. Slowly. Hesitantly. It was Maleshoane. She had a purple blanket on her shoulder. She was holding a stick, which is normally accoutrement for men, not for women. Even from this distance I could see that it was the beaded type, the one with many bright colours.

Moliehi looked at me and smiled. I did not smile back. I did not want Maleshoane to think that I was happy to see her. Though I had told Moliehi that she would be back.

O leshano. She is lying, I had said. She will be back.

A time to mourn, and a time to dance.

Oh no, that is not how we do it. The Word needs some correction there. It is always a time to dance. We are Basotho. We dance whether we are sad or whether we are happy. Dance is not only an expression of joy. It is an expression of life. We mourn through dance. We dance for the dead.

Midway down the escarpment Maleshoane stopped. And sat down on the grass.

Let me go and welcome her, said Moliehi. Make sure your brakes are tight. We don't want a runaway wheelchair at a funeral.

I didn't know why she wanted to make it her business to welcome her.

The last time I saw Maleshoane was at the hospital. At Baragwanath. She came with Mochini-oa-Ipommpa to tell me that Mohalalitoe was on the run for a couple of weeks but was now in jail. He was asking that I should forgive him, he was taken over by his heart, and didn't have any intention of shooting me.

And after I forgive him will I be able to walk again? I asked. Will Noria come back to life again? You know that her body still lies in the

218

mortuary. Are we going to see it wake up from there and go to look for the child of my mother in Lesotho?

After Mochini left, Maleshoane beseeched me not to give up all we had built. The Cult of the Arum-Lily would not be there without us, as it was our music that had brought about its huge following. Mochini was willing to work under my leadership to take the movement to great heights. It was important that we did not give up, especially now that the Cult of the Train was in disarray, its leaders on the wanted posters, leaving a gap that we must fill.

Are you aware that I do not have feet? I asked.

But you do have feet, she said. There.

They are dead, Shoane. I can't walk.

You are a very strong man, she said. You will walk. You will be healed and walk. The Cult of the Arum-Lily has some of the best traditional healers and diviners. They will make you walk. Think about it. Think of the music we will produce without the greedy Mohalalitoe. Think of all the mines we will own.

None of the famo gangs own those mines, Shoane, I pleaded. Everybody is there illegally. I am like this because of those mines. I am not going back there.

A few days later she came with a bunch of flowers. Shoane and flowers was a ridiculous sight. She also brought a packet of fish and chips which I was sure she bought at the taxi rank just outside the hospital's main gate.

She pleaded with me again about carrying forward the great tradition of the Flower. I supposed that was why she brought me flowers; it was a show-and-tell attempt. She tried to take me on a guilt trip, back to the time when we performed at Victoria Hotel with Mme Mpuse and I invited her to join me. She left everything that was going for her to join my band. She was a happy freelance dancer in great

219

demand with various bands and I made her leave all that. And now I wanted to dump her in Johannesburg without anything to her name. At least, if we went back to Mohalalitoe, the group, we would take over ownership of the band and rebuild from what Mohalalitoe, the man, had destroyed. We would be our own bosses. Even Mochini would be our employee if we played our cards smartly.

You cannot do this to me, she said. Don't think only of yourself.

Are you aware that you didn't even ask after my health? I asked.

Oh, sorry, how's your health?

This really annoyed me. She was more interested in the riches and fame we would lose if we gave up our share of the Cult of the Arum-Lily than in anything else, including us as human beings. I told her I did not want to see her again.

Take your flowers with you, I said. People will laugh at me with all these flowers next to my bed.

She left. I never saw her again. That was weeks ago.

The only people who continued to visit me that whole month were Tau ea Khale and his grandchildren. When I told him that after my discharge we would bury Noria in my home village in Lesotho he wanted to come. But I told him it would be difficult. I had no intention of ever returning to Gauteng again. I was sad to hear of Tau ea Khale's passing a few weeks later and regretted that I had not come with him to Likhoele when he had offered. I felt that he would have left some blessings. He would also have something to tell my father in that world of no return, that I did try to get his remains from the White man's mine. That he shouldn't be too angry with me, my mishaps happened in the process of righting the wrongs.

As for Maleshoane, Moliehi did not believe me when I told her she would return. And now there she was, sitting on the ground on the incline, talking animatedly with the child of my mother.

A time to scatter stones and a time to gather them, a time to embrace and a time to refrain from embrace, a time to search and a time to give up.

Toloki spoke. He did not bother to make his face presentable. He spoke. In words not in wails. Not in screams.

The preacherman's book is telling the truth, he said.

Is he the Nurse? I heard a woman ask a few feet from my wheelchair. It is proper that he be the Nurse since he was the husband of the deceased woman, after all.

He can't be the Nurse, said another woman. They say he was not there when it happened. He had abandoned his wife and left for overseas.

But what I heard, said the third one, boy-child is the one who stole his wife. When she was shot the pherese famo musicians were fighting over her with boy-child.

They discussed me as if I were not there. As if I were a piece of meat. But I did not bother correcting them. Where would I end if I were to correct every gossip in Likhoele?

The preacherman's book is talking of me, continued Toloki. Scattering and gathering stones. Embracing and saying goodbye. Searching. But not giving up. I do not give up. I am in search of mourning. More so than ever now that I have mourned the love of my life. I am not the Nurse at this funeral but the mourner. Not only in my professional capacity. I am the bereaved, whatever the circumstances of our taking different paths lately may be. I was wandering among murdered saints in northern England when the message reached me that Noria was murdered. Thank you, boy-child, for remembering to inform me.

Toloki's anguish hit me very hard. I wondered how Moliehi felt. Maybe that's why she was not returning to the proceedings.

Maleshoane gave her a good excuse to escape. And be as far away from these tears as possible.

Toloki's face was a mess. A gentleman gave him a handkerchief. He wiped his face and blew his nose. He handed the handkerchief back to the owner. The gentleman withdrew his hand instead of reaching for the handkerchief. It fell into the gaping grave.

Maybe it is all for the better, said Toloki. My tears will be buried with Noria.

Some people chuckled.

Thank you, boy-child, for remembering me, he repeated. I am going to sit here and mourn for the rest of the day, and for the whole night. In the morning I will depart once more, never to be seen in these parts again. My searching for mourning is very long and will take me to many places. Vuka, Noria! Vuka, sihambe! Or I will erase all the years I was with you. They did not exist. Both the bad and the beautiful. All of two decades must go. It is for me to take the time back, to erase time itself and start my journey in search of mourning from the beginning of the millennium. That's where my story will begin from now onwards. Of course, Noria will not be with me even though I will have reversed the time. She is here now in this grave. She is dead. She cannot reverse her time. Only I can reverse mine. I will therefore be by myself in my wanderings.

It was all so convoluted; none of us understood what Toloki was now talking about. But I was not bothered. After all, the man was a professional mourner, a profession none of us knew existed, he was therefore entitled to talk in riddles if it made him feel better.

Even as we washed our hands in aloed water after the coffin had been lowered and the grave filled with soil and rocks placed on the mound, those among us who were curious to know things that were not their business continued to debate what his words meant. They could not ask him to explain because he remained sitting on Noria's grave mumbling memories and litanies.

Later that day when everyone had gone back to their homes Moliehi and Maleshoane took a plate of samp and meat and a billy-can of sorghum beer to Toloki. They said he did not acknowledge them. He continued with his mourning. They hoped stray dogs would not end up eating that food.

He was waffling, I said to Moliehi. Grief has made him have delusions.

It is my grief too, she said. But he is too selfish to recognise that. He behaves as if he is the only one who has lost something.

But no one stopped you from declaring your grief at the grave-side, I said.

I do not need to declare anything to anyone, said Moliehi. I do not need to show off. It is enough that Noria is lying next to my mother.

You are angry, I said.

I cannot be angry with people who are alive just because the one I love is dead.

I left to talk with Maleshoane, to find out why she came back.

*

Hymns have dried in my mouth. They are still there in my heart. They never leave the heart. The mouth refuses to spew them out even when the crowds at concerts demand them. Even when they shout my praises, oh boy-child, kabela manong, boy-child, the one who will be divvied by vultures, stand up and sing 'U Ka Se Nqete'. Have they cowed you down, boy-child? Have the bullets of gang-sters stolen your voice? Did your hymns go with your legs? Are you filled with fear, boy-child? Are you afraid to sing "Mampoli'?

They know the truth. They just like to tease. They know that 'U Ka Se Nqete' is a song of the past. It is a song that was inspired by

Tau ea Khale, the living ancestor who lives no more. He left to join his dead colleagues more than a year ago. Peacefully in his sleep. The song carries within itself memories that are too raw to stoke. It carries his words. But it also reminds me that when it was composed from the words of the living ancestor I was on a quest for my father. And his bones still lie buried in a mineshaft.

As for ''Mampoli', it is still relevant today because its issues have not been resolved; the murder accused are still the murder accused, and the people of the Train, the legendary icons as newspapers write of them, still feature on *Wanted* posters and Facebook postings: *Wanted for murder, attempted murder, and conspiracy to murder and malicious damage to property*. But we are no longer interested. Ha re sa li kena. Their fate is no longer tied to our fate.

Now it is Moliehi they talk about. Moliehi, child of my mother, is a kheleke of the world. It does not matter where we play. It can be at someone's feast in Matelile, a famo party in Thabana Morena, a concert in a township hall in Bloemfontein, a poolside party at a hotel in Maseru, Moliehi, child of my mother, is the kheleke everyone wants to hear.

Though my mouth ran dry of hymns from the day a bullet from Mohalalitoe's gun lodged itself in my spine, which is where it still is to this day, my fingers' dexterity has not been lost. It shows itself in full flight on the accordion. And Moliehi, child of my mother, will sing her hymns to no one else's accordion but mine. As soon as Maleshoane pushes me onto the stage in my wheelchair, and the drumbeat threatens to awaken even my dead limbs, the accordion, as if of its own accord, rends the audience's collective liver. And Moliehi's seoeleoeleleeeee cuts through the diaphragm to compound the damage.

Maleshoane's dance steps sweep through the stage, from one end to the other. Sometimes she is brandishing a beaded stick like a man of war, and sometimes, depending on the song, she is just vibrating her breasts and buttocks as if reacting to the snows of the Maluti Mountains. Like me, she no longer sings the hymns of the wanderers. She only dances. Often, she performs the very dances full of sorrow and sometimes full of humour that she used to perform for Mme Mpuse, and later for Mohalalitoe, before she imagined herself a kheleke in her own right. Now she performs them for Moliehi's hymns.

As for Maleshoane's own hymns, she claimed her words went dry when mine did. Her hymns were only good as a foil to mine. Without mine she had nothing to respond to. So, she dances all night long, without ever getting tired, and without losing an ounce of her weight despite all that exercise.

I don't buy it. I mean, that her words went dry. I suspect this is just an excuse. I suspect that Shoane will one day burst out into the self-deprecating hymn singer she had become in the Land of Gold. She had shown the flair and had composed some of the best freestyle lines in our performances together. Perhaps she did not want to create bad blood by challenging Moliehi in her position as the leading singer of hymns. Or maybe she knew she would only be second best if she tried to compete. So, she would rather leave the singing to Moliehi, at least for now.

Maleshoane manages the group. She has a better head for business than the two of us. She is more ambitious too. Whereas all we want, me and Moliehi, all we want is to make ourselves happy by spreading happiness, Maleshoane dreams of bigger things for us. Stardom that surpasses that of Mme Mpuse, of 'Malitaba before her, of deadly men such as Mahlanya and Lekase, without the madness of gangland warfare. And she is bent on making that dream a reality.

I tell her that she is old fashioned if she still benchmarks us with those hymn singers of older generations. There are new voices now. Youngsters who have taken our idiom that was basically based on rural Lesotho culture and mine culture – the culture of trains and compounds and stick fighting – and have given it a modern urban twist. I am talking of bad ugly dogs like Skoen Pampiri who, though hailing from the Eastern Cape, is of the Sesotho tradition. His music is closer to our idiom. Another one who is closer to us because his rhythms and melodies still conform to those of the singers of the hymns of the wanderers is Malome Vector.

Your own uncle? asks Maleshoane, as she manoeuvres our old Mazda van on the gravel road on our way to the camp where we are booked to play at Hotel Mafeteng.

Malome means Uncle in Sesotho.

How come I have never heard of this uncle? asks Moliehi.

She doesn't like to talk much. In all our trips she leaves the jab-bering to me and Maleshoane. She says she wants to preserve her voice for better things – singing the hymns of the wayfarers for an appreciative audience.

You people are so ignorant, I say. Malome is his name. But he is not the only one. I have listened to a woman called Irysh Da Princess. And don't start asking if she is King Letsie's daughter. It is just her name.

That's what you do when you no longer have legs to walk to places of mischief; you listen to all this music by people with strange names, Maleshoane says.

It will do you a lot of good if you listen to them too. This one is called Ntate Stunna. He is my favourite of all the new voices. His accordion is still the famo accordion, but with more sophistication.

I play Ntate Stunna's song on my phone.

I am missing home. I am missing home. I am missing home.

Ke hopotse hae. Mokhotlong Thialala. Where you draw water with your nail.

Maleshoane breaks out laughing and Moliehi chuckles.

You don't appreciate all this beauty? I am stunned. The song is truly moving.

He repeats the same thing over and over again, that he is missing his home, says Maleshoane. Has his poetry run out of words?

It is for the rhythm, Shoane. For the beat. Remember this is modern music, drawing its influences not only from our hymns, but from rap music. Like our hymns, this man praises his town and village, Mokhotlong, Thialala. And then he praises himself. Just like our hymns. In one of his hymns he says he is as tough as iron and is a great kheleke. Exactly like our tradition where we boast of our prowess, the beauty of our villages and our sisters. It *is* our tradition in fact, rendered in a modern idiom. Remember, our elders say a new shield is stencilled from an old one.

I think it is beautiful music, Maleshoane admits. But some of us are traditionalists. Our tradition is forever. These new ones, you will not hear of them tomorrow. They are like bubblegum that you chew and then the sweetness runs out.

What you call our tradition hasn't always been like this, I say. It changed in the process. Nothing stays the same forever and ever. Our grandfathers played the concertina and sang the hymns differently. Then they played the organ. We play the accordion. Some of us, like Mme Mpuse, added guitars and saxophones and the like. These brave young people, I hope they will still be here tomorrow. If not them, those they have influenced. A new kind of world music can come out of this, judging from their talent. If I were still a hymn singer, I would learn this new style. I would sing my hymns to this kind of music. I would not rhyme though.

227

But that is the most beautiful part of their music, says Maleshoane.

Yes, of course it is beautiful the way they do it. They rhyme because their roots are also in hip hop. The roots of my hymns are in the lithoko poetry, and that doesn't rhyme. Or it's not meant to traditionally. Big boys don't rhyme.

I do not know anything of what you people are talking about, says Moliehi.

You need to listen to more of these young disrupters, Moliehi, I answer. We can learn a lot from these beautiful boys and girls. That would help us to stay relevant.

I don't want to stay relevant. I want to sing the hymns of the wanderers the way boy-child, son of my father, used to sing them. I am boy-child incarnate.

I am here, I say. I am not dead yet.

She reminded me of the things we used to talk about during my rehab. She was down-spirited like me, saying she could not sing without Noria and therefore she was giving up the life of a molelere. After all, it was Noria who had turned her into a performer. It was she who had more faith in her than she had in herself, which gave her confidence to go on stage. Without Noria she was nothing and could not go on.

I told her she was talking nonsense. It was not Noria but Moliehi herself I saw taking an audience of ruffians by the scruff of their collective neck one night in Durban Deep. She could do it without Noria. She could even do it *for* Noria.

But you hated my singing, she said.

I was a fool then, I said. I was too protective. Now it is your turn to be protective towards me. And by the way, I didn't hate your singing. You have no idea what your singing can do. I have. You must sing, Moliehi, child of my mother. You must sing.

228

And she sang. Toddling steps at first. But in no time she was in her element. Her voice was making grown men cry. Her words turned women into streams of ululation.

It is a relay. I will complete the race for you, she said after one great performance.

The end is always a journey.

Acknowledgements

Thanks to Sebonomoea Ramainoane, founder and owner of Mo-Afrika FM, *Mo-Afrika* newspaper, singer of accordion music and saxophonist, beekeeper, sheep farmer, pastor and village chief, great multi-tasker, for his in-depth knowledge of the music and political culture of Lesotho and the deadly conflicts of musicians, illegal mining gangs and politicians. Thank you to the real-life accordion musicians of the famo genre whose music and lyrics informed a lot of my story. These include Famole, Mantša, Puseletso Seema, Khosi Mosotho Chakela and Lekhotla la Terene, Letlama and its various incarnations, Mahlanya, Lekase and others. I thank my son, Neo Ndukumfa Solomzi Mda, who read each chapter as I churned it out and made valuable predictive comments. Other useful readers were Mathe VK Ntšekhe, Elelwani Netshifhire, David Shriver, Irene Ada, Geri Lipschultz, Annicia Manyaapelo and Maboreng Maharaswa. I also salute my long-time editor, Pam Thornley.

Also by Zakes Mda

The Zulus of New York

The Great Farini would stride on to the stage and announce, 'Ladies and gentlemen, and now for the highlight of the day, the ferocious Zulus.'

The impresario Farini introduced Em-Pee and his troupe to his kind of show business, and now they must earn their bread. In 1885 in a bustling New York City, they are the performers who know the true Zulu dances, while all around them fraudsters perform silly jigs.

Reports on the Anglo-Zulu War portrayed King Cetshwayo as infamous, and audiences in London and New York flock to see his kin. What the gawking spectators don't know is that Em-Pee once carried nothing but his spear and shield, when he had to flee his king.

But amid the city's squalid vaudeville acts appears a vision that leaves Em-Pee breathless: in a cage in Madison Square Park is Acol, a Dinka princess on display. For Em-Pee, it is love at first sight, though Acol is not free to love anyone back.

Little Suns

'There are many suns,' he said. 'Each day has its own. Some are small, some are big. I'm named after the small ones.'

It is 1903. A lame and frail Malangana – 'Little Suns' – searches for his beloved Mthwakazi after many lonely years spent in Lesotho. Mthwakazi was the young woman he had fallen in love with twenty years earlier, before the assassination of Hamilton Hope ripped the two of them apart.

Intertwined with Malangana's story, is the account of Hope – a colonial magistrate who, in the late nineteenth century, was undermining the local kingdoms of the eastern Cape in order to bring them under the control of the British. It was he who wanted to coerce Malangana's king and his people, the amaMpondomise, into joining his battle – a scheme Malangana's conscience could not allow.

Zakes Mda's novel *Little Suns* weaves the true events surrounding the death of Magistrate Hope into a touching story of love and perseverance that can transcend exile and strife.